Other works

First published by Half Wing Press in 2017

Print ISBN: 978-0-9988504-4-3
Ebook ISBN: 978-0-9988504-5-0

For more about the author visit www.JChateau.com or www.Facebook.com/JonathanChateauAuthor.

THE DEATH WISH GAME

A NOVEL

JONATHAN CHATEAU

To my good friend, Grant, who has made this book what it is today. Thanks for your feedback and for reading the first few drafts...

More than once.

"Be ye angry, and sin not: let not the sun go down on your wrath."
— *Ephesians 4:26*

"One day your life will flash before your eyes. Make sure it's worth watching."
— *Gerard Way*

1

Road Trip

I'm jarred awake by the bus slamming on its brakes. Are we there yet? I open my eyes. At first, everything is blurry. Then the bus cabin comes into focus. The interior lights are all off. It's dark outside. We've stopped moving.

Something about this feels incredibly wrong.

I start to rise—but I'm stuck.

I look down.

My entire body is wrapped in . . . duct tape?

What the hell?

"It's party time, people!" a deep voice says from the front of the cabin. I can't make out who it is. "Hope you all are nice and snug in your seats. I tend to go a little tight on the restraints."

Restraints?

I wriggle in my seat. Yeah, I'm not going anywhere. It's hard enough trying to breathe let alone move.

"Shit's about to get real"—the man laughs—"real quick."

What is going on?

Is this a joke?

This isn't real. It's surreal. I must be dreaming. I mean, the last time I'd been on a bus, I wasn't literally strapped to my seat in a cabin full of strangers crying and pissing themselves. I was on my way back home from aikido summer camp. Not the kind of kiddie summer camp that involves bonfires, volleyball, and social bonding, but a rather intense week of martial-arts training for grown-ups.

***

I was testing for my black belt.

Years of training had all led up to this point.

There were lots of joint locks, arm bars, elbow pins, and face-plants into the sweat-soaked mat. It reeked of rubber and feet. Even though the camp was held in an air-conditioned college gymnasium, it felt more like a sauna. Must've had at least twenty pounds of perspiration soaked into my gi alone. One of my training partners, Phil, was a walking rainforest. He was perpetually drenched, which kind of worked to his advantage in a disgusting sort of way. Couldn't grab hold of him to perform a wrist lock to save my life. It was like trying to snatch hold of a fish that knew how to dodge, counter, and plow me into the cushioned canvas floor.

When summer camp was over, Phil ended up sitting next to me on the bus. Told me he owed me a beer considering how many times he drove my head into the ground. I'm sure if we had practiced one more day, the imprint of my face would've been permanently embedded into the mat like some archaic stone relief. I thanked him for not going easy on me. For coming at me full force, in a real-life kick-your-ass kind of way. I didn't want to be handed a black belt. I never wanted to be a paper tiger with a certificate of achievement that meant nothing on the street. A certificate would never hold up to a sucker punch to the face.

Fortunately, I was able to power through the nerves. Ignore the room full of eyes, of fellow students, teachers, and family who had come from all around the state to see who would pass and who would fail.

I managed to sink into the moment and counter Phil's strikes with everything I had learned over the years. A dance of skill against a wild opponent. I performed this all under the watchful, stoic gaze of some of aikido's best sensei.

A blur of motion, Phil came at me from every angle, and somehow my lizard brain processed this, and I turned his momentum against him.

Somehow, I survived the test.

Somehow, I earned myself a black belt.

It felt surreal when I stepped off the mat. I had achieved the belt through sheer determination. By not giving up. Something I have forgotten in the years since aikido camp. That's what's led me to my current fate.

Phil had explained to me that a black belt was not an end-all. Some students think that's all that training is about. Get the credentials and switch hobbies. But he said that earning a black belt was more akin to getting a diploma than a doctorate. "Rodney, with a black belt," he said, "you're just getting started."

But I had to explain to him that earning a black belt was a side effect of training. I told him the real reason I trained was that it was my way of coping with stress—namely the pressure of managing people and meeting the constant needs of my boss. I've always been a reluctant leader. My star sign is Aries, so maybe by default that positioned me to have to lead in life. I'd like to think that's why I took up martial arts—so that I could mold myself into a better man. A stronger leader. Build up my self-confidence.

Phil told me he trained because around eight years ago he was jumped at a bar in downtown Columbia. Several thugs were hiding in the parking lot, waiting for their next intoxicated victim. That was Phil. He never saw them coming. They beat the shit out of him, took his money, his watch, and most importantly a gold ring with a garnet gemstone. A ring his deceased daughter had given him. He swore after that he would never lose a fight again. And that's why he's trained and trained and trained. He said that an ancient Greek poet once said it best: "One does not rise to the level of their expectations, but falls to the level of their training."

"Socrates?" I'd asked.

"Archilochus," he answered, with a slight smile.

"Or maybe, in the words of Mike Tyson," I said, "everyone's got a plan until they get punched in the mouth. That's why we train, right?"

We both shared a good laugh. Yeah, that was a pretty epic summer. I was happy and had more money in the bank than I knew what to do with. And I was single.

Fast forward a decade.

I'm newly divorced, unemployed, and have a complete and utter understanding of what it means to be at rock bottom—and once you get to that awful place, a lot of things have a way of not mattering anymore. The petty things you stressed over—the deadlines, the perfectly crafted emails, the quarterly reviews, doing the dishes, not forgetting anniversaries or birthdays, remembering to put the seat down—none of that shit really matters.

When you hit rock bottom, you have the privilege of walking around and giving the world the middle finger. You might just find yourself wanting to implode. Irrationally taking responsibility for every negative event, every outcome. When emotions have taken the driver's seat of your brain, logic is hard to separate from any ounce of rationality.

When you hit rock bottom, things are tasteless, joyless, and a dark haze of depression sets over your vision, peeling, cracking, and obscuring your view like a bad tint job. When you've gone that deep, that far down, scraping off that layer of misery requires more than Windex and razor blades.

Although the razor blades might work. Or a gun. My father's old Beretta would do the trick. He gifted it to me not long before he passed. Told me to use it for self-defense.

So, self-defense it is.

I'm saving me from myself.

6

This morning I woke up. Had myself a Belgian waffle. Then put the business end of the Beretta in my mouth and counted to ten.

1 . . .

2 . . .

The barrel had a tangy, acrid taste.

3 . . .

I'd assumed batteries tasted the same.

4 . . .

I was surprised at how much my body was shaking.

5 . . .

6 . . .

It was as if there was an internal struggle going on. That primordial need to live, to survive, being overridden by my depression. By that bad tint job installed into my brain by those who had caused me pain.

7 . . .

As my tongue flicked across the 9mm diameter opening of my gun barrel, I understood why every sad song in the world was written. I understood how those artists felt.

8 . . .

Those artists weren't looking for Grammys or platinum records. They were seeking to fill that void in their heart. A black hole of nothingness, of feeling meaningless.

9 . . .

I mumbled a quick, "Forgive me, Father," because most likely I was going to Hell.

Though I never got to find out.

My sister, Becky, called at the right time. Always had a knack for being timely. Told me she bought me a bus ticket to Miami. She told me I could start over and move in with her.

Start over?

She went on about missing me and wanting to reconnect. Little did she know that a Beretta was sitting on my lap and that a few seconds earlier I was about to attempt to replicate a Pollock painting using the backside of my skull and a lot of red and gray matter.

As she continued talking, my brain shifted from self-pity to a glimmer of . . . well, hope.

I figured, why not?

What did I have to lose at this point? I'd already lost the very things that defined me—my management career and my woman.

Now I had the liberty of saying screw the dishes and birthdays.

Newsflash, boss-man: This job sucks.

Managing your lazy employees sucks. Your paisley ties suck. No one cares that you were at Woodstock. Nothing was ever good enough for you. Not the overtime. Not the times I had to come in from vacation to keep our department afloat. Or when I was cornered into choosing you over spending time with my wife—

Not that it had mattered anyway since she left me.

Still, nothing was good enough for you. You promoted the green-eyed, busty brunette who just so happened to be a Florida Gator—ha, ha, ha. The two of you at the water cooler, talking about UF, football, and a mutual love for all things Crate and Barrel.

Yeah, I know why I was let go.

Because there was only room enough for one. And I didn't have the right parts.

Apparently, I didn't have the right parts for either my boss or my ex-wife, Diane.

She upgraded. Found better, fitter parts on her personal trainer's body. Dude's name was Chad. I know this because I introduced them. He'd been my personal trainer first. Then I made the mistake of hooking up the two of them since she had nagged me about getting in shape herself, even though I was completely OK with every inch of her frame. Connecting them was a fitness decision that I would forever regret.

Chad.

Screw you, Chad.

I've never met a Chad I liked.

All of the Chads I've known have been car salesmen, lawyers, or mortgage brokers. They've all had chips on their shoulders and thought they were God's gift to whatever profession they were in. This Chad had been no different. I saw the sparkle in her eye when they first met. I should've picked up on it. That twinkle in her eye, that glimmer I hadn't seen since our first few dates.

Diane did this thing she did with her lip when she gets hot and bothered. A subtle lip curl, generally on the right side.

Diane plus Chad had equaled a lip curl that day.

I'd been too naive to pick up on it.

Or stupid blind.

Suddenly she was at the gym way more often than she'd used to be. I'd thought it was due to some mid-year resolution she hadn't told me about. When I finally asked her about her aggressive fitness regimen that had seemed to blossom out of nowhere, an argument erupted. I was accused of being insecure and unsupportive. Far from the truth. I just had this blip on my worry radar that kept telling me something was not right.

Radars rarely lie.

Well, at least not in my experience. I guess I should've seen the correlation between Diane's increasingly fit physique and her diminishing sex drive. Turns out, her sex drive didn't decrease at all. It had just shifted to a new partner.

Then the divorce struck me like a stake to the heart.

Mr. and Mrs. Corso no more.

Thanks, Chad.

Screw you, Chad.

My cold Beretta in my mouth.

A fire of deceit and hate in my heart.

Yeah, Becky called me at the right time. She's the only one who has ever given a damn about me. She'd never cared for Diane. Initially, I'd thought that Becky was simply jealous of a woman stealing her brother's time, but it turns out she was just protecting her older brother from his snake of a wife.

When Becky didn't come to our wedding, I was pissed. Didn't talk to her for years after that. Since the divorce, though, we've reconnected. I apologized for my stupid behavior and for not talking to her, and for not listening. Even though she had made her protest apparent by not being there for the exchange of vows, Becky hadn't been wrong.

I owe my life to her.

Literally.

She works two jobs and is putting herself through college. Dreams of being a dentist. All the woman does is work and study, work and study. She scrounged up enough money to get me from South Carolina to Florida. I'd had to sell my dream car, my Dodge Challenger, to afford the legal fees.

Divorce is an expensive beast.

Financially, physically and mentally.

Drove me to put a gun in my mouth.

Becky had been excited to tell me that she'd gotten a deal on a bus ticket, some discount bus line I never heard of called Mane's Transportation. She said they'd received stellar customer reviews from several websites.

Still, it's incredibly humbling to be on a bus, with total strangers, and not driving in the comfort of my own car.

When I first got on the bus, I'd noticed that it had an odd smell to it. The piercing, spiced aroma of flea market patchouli permeated the air. My first thought was that maybe the previous passengers had been a bunch of granola-heads from Berkley or Asheville. Then again, the tired and dated exterior of the bus suggested it had seen many years of service on the road. The stale smell inside wasn't really that much of a surprise. Perhaps the incense was just a lazy way of attempting to mask the musty odor embedded in the seat cushions and carpeting.

As I found my seat, I'd noticed that very few people made eye contact with me, which was perfectly fine. I wasn't here to make friends.

I was on this bus to get back to Florida.

To reconnect with my sister. To start over. To escape the depression and the bad memories and the places that I'd used to visit with Diane.

Columbia, South Carolina. My once beautiful hometown, now a city of constant reminders of loss.

When the bus driver had finally shown up, he'd looked like a misplaced biker.

Scratch that.

He resembled a misplaced Viking. The man was almost seven feet tall. A thick, gray spider web of a beard covered most of his face. He had a black newsboy cap, like the trademark hat worn by Brian Johnson of AC/DC. His eyes were hollow; beady black pits that sized us up as if we were going to fight him in a boxing ring.

When he spoke, his voice was even deeper than I expected.

"Thanks for choosing Mane's Transportation for your trip to Miami." As he talked, I could barely see his lips through his beard. "My name's Jim Grimm. To set the ground rules, I don't tolerate fighting, and there are no weapons allowed on the bus. Is anyone carrying?"

I had snuck my pocket knife on board. Carry it with me wherever I go. It had brought me luck in the past. The times I didn't have it on me—my last week at work and when I introduced Diane to Jerk-face—the results spoke for themselves.

I'd had it on me when I was about to kill myself.

So it's on me now.

In answer to his question, a few passengers mumbled no.

Jim went on to explain that Mane's Transportation goes beyond what other bus lines offer. "Even though all of you got cheap tickets, the cheapest tickets available, that doesn't mean that we skimp on quality."

Jim moved his head slowly, from side to side, making eye contact with every single person on the bus, seemingly memorizing and reading our faces the way I imagined a secret service agent would.

His tone was flat; a tour guide who's delivered this speech a thousand times before. "But before we head out, we'll be feasting like kings and queens." And he stepped off the bus, disappeared for ten minutes, leaving the passengers craning their necks, mumbling to one another.

When he returned, he had two coolers in his hands. He dropped them down onto the aisle and kicked them toward us with his boot.

"This one has prime rib sandwiches, chicken wraps, and veggie wraps." He pointed to the other cooler. "This one's got beers, soda, and vitamin water for those of you who are health conscious."

Some of the passengers smiled, traded excited glances with one another.

"Like I said, Mane's Transportation goes above and beyond," he said. "It's a long trip, and the first meal is on us."

People rose from their seats and took turns picking out their meals.

"We'll make only one stop on the way to Miami, so this meal ought to hold you all until then." The way Jim spoke made me uneasy. As if we didn't have a choice in the matter. Almost as if he were delivering orders to his troops. No weapons. Eat this. One stop on the way.

Weird, but whatever.

I was hungry.

And eager to start a new life.

So I knelt down next to the cooler, chose the prime rib and grabbed a beer. Free food on my trip out of this town of regret? Not a bad start to the day.

As I rose, I could feel Jim's eyes on me. We shared an awkward moment of silence, followed by me thanking him.

Not a shred of emotion on his face. Not a smile. Not a frown. Just a fuzzy face with wrinkles, and brown eyes that seemed to be saying more than he was letting on. He then nodded, settled into his seat, and played with his cell phone.

I wasted no time tearing into that sandwich. To my surprise, it tasted like heaven. The bread and meat melted in my mouth. The beer was the perfect temperature. Can't tell you the last time I'd derived joy from food and drink, but there it was. Some magical ingredient in these refreshments made me feel a little bit . . . happy. Brought a tingle of peace. Between the food and the travel, the idea of a fresh start initially inspired a sense of hope.

Boy, was I wrong.

Soon, Jim, had us sliding out of the bus station and onto the highway. And it wasn't long before the sandwich, the comfort of the chair, and the flood of emotions knocked me out.

***

But I didn't awaken in my new home in Miami. I was roused by muffled screams, groans, and a deep voice yelling, "Come on! Wake up, people!"

And that's when I find myself strapped to my seat.

The cabin lights flicker on. The windows mirror our own panicked expressions against the blackness of night outside. Can't tell where we're at. The bus isn't moving. We're parked in the middle of who knows where.

Well, Jim did say that we would make one stop before Miami.

But where exactly is this stop?

I blink several times, as my eyes adjust to the lights. Jim comes into focus. He's standing in the aisle, arms propped on the seats to either side of him. "I said, EVERYBODY," he yells, "WAKE THE FUCK UP!"

Everyone around me is stuck in their chairs, too. I try to move once again, but the tape has got me strapped down to my seat, good and secure. There's duct tape on my mouth as well. This is either a prank or a real-life nightmare. For a moment, I question if this is a dream, but the distinct, bitter taste of glue from the tape seeps into my mouth. No dream.

"Like I said," Jim says, "it's party time!"

Oh, my God.

What is going on?

13

"When I said that Mane's isn't like other bus lines, I meant that when you ride with us, you generally don't get to where you're going." He chuckles in a self-amused sort of way. As if there's an inside joke somewhere that we're not in on. "Did you all enjoy the complimentary food and drinks? They were served up with complimentary sedatives."

A few of the passengers' cries are stifled—seems their mouths all taped shut as well.

"Wonderful. You're no doubt wondering what's going on. Well, I'll tell you." He pauses, trades glances with everyone as if taking attendance. "You're part of our game now. There are eyes on every one of you. Your savior is curious to find out who might last the night and reach the finish line. Unfortunately, most don't. Those lucky few who have survived, have a whole new appreciation for their lives. I'm living proof."

With that, Jim, pulls up his T-shirt, revealing a chest with ripples of pink and beige scars. Looks as though he got into a fight with a bear and only just escaped.

"The rules are simple," he says. "Follow the flares to reach the safe zone. Make it there, and you live. There will be a truck waiting to take you back to your cubicles, reality TV, and Facebook news feeds." He then shrugs. "Stay, and they will come tear you apart."

Some of the people cry, some scream through their duct tape, some whimper.

Jim pauses. His gaze falls on one of the passengers. Someone with oily, black hair shaped in a bowl cut. "Aww. Poor thing. Your mascara is running." He leans toward him. "You must be frightened. As you should be." Jim checks his watch, then looks back at us. "It's midnight. They'll be here soon."

Outside a truck pulls up.

"Well . . . that's my ride. Good luck, and thanks for traveling with Mane's!" Jim rushes out, hops into the truck, and it speeds off, leaving us alone, strapped down inside this giant coffin, waiting for God knows what.

2

Flies in the Web

It's one thing to want to take your own life. It's another when some asshole believes he gets to make that decision for you.

The way I'm tied down to this seat, you'd think that we're on a rocket ship headed for the moon. Not even gravity could screw with us. This bus could roll over several times, and all that would escape these chairs would be loose change and crumbs.

This has got to be a prank.

Maybe something my sister set up? Doubtful. Seems awful elaborate given Becky's slim budget and the fact that she's super busy. I don't see how she could pull this off.

A woman up front screams so loudly the duct tape on her mouth does little to suppress it. There are some people sobbing, struggling in their seats. Flies stuck on fly paper. There's a fifty-year-old man next to me, fighting against his restraints. He pauses, looks at me for a moment, eyes brimming with fear. He's on the verge of crying. That dreadful look in his eyes is an unwelcome confirmation that this might just be for real.

Whatever we inadvertently got ourselves into is no joke. It's someone's sick game, all right.

Jim's game.

But why didn't he stick around?

Because he knows what's coming, apparently.

But what?

I wriggle in my seat to find I have a little bit of wiggle room, just enough to slide my hand from being pinned behind my back. Jim, or whoever tied us up, did so in a hurry. Though I mean it when I say there's just a little bit of wiggle room. Between the tightness of my restraints and my jeans, I barely manage to slide my fingers into my pocket.

I bring my leg up, sink my hip down, and push my fingers deeper, feeling for the very tip of my knife, which is tucked deep inside my pocket.

"OH, MY GOD!" A woman up front, probably the same woman who was screaming earlier, has somehow gotten the duct tape off her mouth. "WE ARE GOING TO DIE! SOMEBODY, PLEASE HELP US!" She's shouting this as if the dozen or so other passengers in this bus are in any better a position to do anything themselves.

Well, I'm working on it.

Just . . .

Got . . .

To . . .

Get . . . my . . . fingertip . . .

"SOMEBODY, PLEASE!" And then the woman breaks down, scream-ing and balling her eyes out. It doesn't help the situation at all, I'll tell you that. I almost wish she still had the duct tape over her mouth, as bad as that sounds. I'm sure everyone else here is shitting their pants, too, so her freaking out is only adding to that.

Actually—wait.

Yeah.

Someone did just shit their pants.

And someone peed their pants. There's a sharp, sour smell of urine, sweat, and feces in the air. I've got to get this knife out of my pocket so that we can get off this bus—

There's an explosion of glass. Something just rocketed through one of the front windshields and lands with a wet thud.

The woman screaming up front is suddenly quiet.

In her place, the man sitting across the aisle from her lets out a muffled screech. His eyes swell, inflating like tiny white balloons, as he watches the woman's head slump over. Something is sticking out from her chest—but what? I can't exactly ask the dude what he's freaking out about because we're all about as conversational as mimes with this air conditioning-grade tape suffocating us.

Still, whatever silenced that woman so abruptly can't be good.

My heart sinks. Adding to the growing fear inside me is a tinge of shame. I feel a little terrible for earlier wishing she'd quiet down. I'd wanted her to stop screaming . . . not die.

Everyone squirms in their seats now, writhing like snakes. All of us in our shiny silver cocoons of tape, desperately trying to break free.

I sink lower . . .

Fingertips reaching . . .

Reaching . . .

Another explosion of glass. Something whizzes above our heads. I can't see where it landed.

OK, back to the knife.

Concentrate.

I look down at my pocket, push my hand as deep as I can, the mouth of the pocket getting jammed between my fingers, and I reach. Then I hear the dude up front with the big eyes let out a muffled whimper. My head snaps up in time to catch him slump over. Blood pooling beneath him.

The quills of an . . . arrow sticking out just above his shoulder.

Is somebody taking potshots at us with a hunting bow?

This can't be real.

This has got to be some well-coordinated prank.

Naturally, I'm not the only one who took notice. There's a heavyset African-American woman in the seat behind the big-eyed guy, who is rocking her head and body so violently, attempting to break free of the tape, that I'm worried she might have a heart attack just trying to get out.

Fear does crazy things to people.

I'm not about to sit around to find out who is getting picked off next. I jam my fingers so deep into my pocket that I feel as though my hand is going to split in half.

But it doesn't.

Instead, I'm able to grab the knife with two fingers, pull it back up and out of my pocket, and slip it into the palm of my hand.

Now the tricky part: getting it open.

I shift from side to side in my seat and, with the knife firmly in my grip, wriggle my hand around behind me to meet my other hand. I work at trying to pull out the blade. Thank God I didn't cut my fingernails this week.

Another arrow flies into the cabin. It impales itself into the seat next to me, narrowly missing the old man. The two of us freeze and share a moment staring at the rough brown shaft of the arrow. It's not from a hunting bow or any contemporary toxophilite's inventory. It's just a regular old stick, a very rudimentary projectile, something a Boy Scout or a survivalist would construct.

Still, it's already proven its effectiveness since, as far as I can tell, ones just like it have already killed two people on the bus.

The old man's gaze shifts from the arrow to me. Face full of sweat. Eyes puffy and pooling with tears. I shoot him back a look that says, Don't worry . . .

I've almost got this knife open.

Come on, fingernails!

Make this happen!

I flick my thumbnail several times against the catch in the blade tip, until finally . . . success!

The blade opens, and I'm already sawing away at my restraints. It's going to take me a few minutes to cut through this, but at least I can get myself free and then start releasing others—

A wave of muted screams and snivels travels down the aisle as another arrow zips into the heart of the bus. I hear a stifled whimper and see the old man writhe in his seat.

A knotted shaft of wood is protruding from his chest.

3

Guardian Angel

I want to tell the old guy to hang in there.

Tell him I'm going to get us out of here.

But my mouth is still taped shut.

And now his head is slumped forward. A waterfall of blood seeps down his chest from where the arrow has pierced his heart. I'm filled with overwhelming dread. My heart beats against my chest as if it were a clenched fist of fear trying to break open my ribcage from the inside out. Having the tape strapped across my mouth makes breathing difficult, particularly since panic is beginning to consume me.

I squeeze my eyes shut. Got to focus.

Come on, Rodney, get your shit together.

Witnessing the old man die so violently in front of me just made this even more real.

Yeah, this is not a joke.

Far from it.

Everyone on this bus has been brought here to be put to death—

Don't focus on that!

I've got to get out of this chair before I'm next!

I open my eyes and begin sawing as quickly as this awkward angle will allow. I cut through enough to free my left hand. I rip at the tape, yanking away every strip as if my life depends on it—because it does—and in a matter of precious minutes, I'm free. Grateful to get to my feet. Never has it felt so good to stand up.

Wait.

Bad idea.

I crouch down. Taking a few deep breaths, I do my best to steady the pounding in my chest. My heart thuds like a war drum. I can feel my blood pressure in my ears. I glance up to find the remaining passengers frantically rocking in their seats, desperately working to loosen the tape keeping them tied to this nightmarish shooting gallery.

Please get us out of here, their eyes scream.

I'm already on it.

There are shards of glass everywhere, crunching beneath my shoes. The thick odor of urine, blood, and feces wafts through the bus. It's unbearable, but the adrenaline pumping through my system seems to be overriding my urge to turn and vomit.

There's a guy with perfect, anchorman-brown hair in the row in front of mine. I kneel next to him, to not make myself an easy target for the arrow-wielding snipers outside, and rip the tape off his mouth.

"Oh God," he says in between breaths. "Dude, you're a lifesaver!"

As I cut away at his tape, I tell him not to thank me yet. We're still on the bus in the middle of who-knows-where with invisible assassins picking us off one by one.

There's a garbled, muffled scream from someone at the front of the bus. A person taking an arrow to the throat.

"JESUS H. CHRIST!" the anchorman shouts in my ear. His words laced with a hint of that poisoned beer lingering on his breath. "WHAT IS GOING ON?"

"Shut up!"

He shoots me an insulted look.

"Now let's try to get your arms out," I say as I free him and pull him down to the ground to kneel next to me. "Watch your hands, guy. There's glass everywhere."

21

"Oh my God!" His eyes swell, lips quivering. His head darts in all directions.

"Hey!" I grab the back of his head and force him to look at me. "What's your name?"

"Wh-wh-what?"

"Your name? What's your name?

"Ch-Ch-Chase." Spittle foams at the corners of his lips. "Chase Patterson."

"OK, Chase," I say as I grab both of his shoulders and squeeze. "Right now we've got to get everyone off this bus and get out of here, wherever here is. Look, I know you're scared. Hey, I'm freaked out, too—"

"You're hiding it well, man—"

"Chase!" I shake him. "Listen, I need you to calm down, all right?"

He nods his head, tears sliding down his cheeks.

"You with me?" I ask.

"Yeah."

"You sure?"

"Yeah-yeah-yeah!"

I peer into his panicked, hazel eyes and am struck with this odd sense of knowing that he's probably going to fall apart, like completely apart, at some point and get himself killed.

Moving along to the next passenger, he and I make quick work of freeing a big, burly dude decked in plaid, sporting a bushy beard. The guy looks like he cuts down whole forests for a living.

"Name's Bear," he says.

Seems like an accurate name.

"Rodney," I say.

Glancing further down the aisle, the African-American woman, shudders, and sobs incessantly. Head bobbing with each wave of tears.

Across from her, the tall teenager with the bowl cut has his head turned toward the window. He's not moving or whimpering or even blinking from what I can see. Not sure if he's dead. Only one way to find out.

"OK, Bear, Chase," I say. "Let's keep moving."

As we make our way single file down the aisle, creeping along on our hands and knees, another arrow whizzes above our heads. Chase shrieks behind me. I look back to see if he's OK. Mouth slung open in fear, a single drop of saliva dangles from his bottom lip.

"You all right?" I ask.

"Yeah-yeah-yeah," he chatters, voice quaking.

I tell Chase and Bear to help the kid with the bowl cut. I nod to the African-American woman. "I'll help her."

Bear gives me a thumbs-up, and we get to work on our respective rescues.

The African-American woman nearly jumps when I place a hand on her lap. She glances down at me with eyes as big as gumballs. Tears pool at the corners of her eyes and then race down her cheeks, over the reflective tape covering her mouth. She's a wet mess of distress, and I can't blame her one bit. I share in her dread. Somehow we have all inadvertently managed to put ourselves in the bowels of something sinister.

"I'm getting us out of here," I tell her as calmly as possible.

Wherever here is.

She nods her head.

I rip the tape off her mouth. She gasps. Through sobs, she tells me, "I just wanna see my babies. Just wanna go home!"

I cut her restraints. "We're going to get you home."

"Please," she says through thick tears, "I just wanna see my babies. I don't know what's going on. Lord, please help us."

I look up at her just as I free her hands from behind her back. I catch a gold cross dangling from her neck, right next to a silver charm with her name engraved on it.

"Liza," I say.

She nods.

"I think the Lord answered." I hold up my pocket knife. "He let me sneak on the bus with this."

She nods again, eyeballs plump with fear. I free her from the chair and yank her down onto the floor—

Just as an arrow pierces her seat. We both watch as it flops up and down like a diving board, then we exchange glances.

"Guess you must have an angel watching over you," I say.

She looks at the arrow again, then back at me. As she wipes the tears from her face and the snot from her nose, she says, "And maybe you're him."

4

What's the Plan?

Bear and Chase free the teenager with the bowl cut and pull him down to the floor. Guess the kid was alive after all. But for someone who just got their ass saved, he doesn't appear very grateful. There's a scowl on his face as though we killed his dog or something.

"You all right?" I ask the kid.

He glances down at his shirt. It's a My Chemical Romance tour shirt. Circa 2007. It's in perfect condition, save for the sweat circles under his arms. Other than that, no wounds. He looks back at me, glaring, almost disappointed to be alive. "Yeppers." Now I see what Jim saw. Mascara. It's running down his face as if he's either been crying, sweating, or both.

"What's your name?" I ask as I feel something stir inside me. A funky vibe. A tingling of my "spider-sense." Aside from everything else going on, there's already something about this kid I don't like. "Well?"

"Introductions? In the middle of a massacre?" The kid laughs to himself in a self-amused sort of way. "Are you retarded or something?"

"If we're going to escape this nightmare," I say, "we're all going to get acquainted pretty quick."

The kid huffs. "I don't want to know you people—"

Bear's hand shoots across the aisle. He grasps the kid's nose and shoves a thumb up into his nostril.

"Ahhhhhhh!" The kid tries to pull away, but Bear's massive hand decides otherwise. "You're hurting me, you chubby hipster!"

"Rodney asked your name," Bear says.

The kid lets out a muffled whimper in response.

An arrow sails right above our head. Everyone watches it fly over us as if we're at some kind of morbid airshow.

Everyone but the three of us.

Our gazes never leave this little punk.

"It only takes nine pounds of pressure to break a nose," Bear says as he leans forward.

Chase glares at Bear with an expression that says, What are you doing? He's a kid!

"Name's Damien, all right!" the kid squeals, his voice nasal. "Now let go!"

"Damien?" Bear raises an eyebrow. "Damien?"

"Yes, fat boy! My name is Damien."

Bear chuckles. "As in Damien . . . the kid from The Omen?"

"I call bullshit," I say. "Bet his real name is Carter or Tanner or something more boring like that."

"Fuck both of you." Damien swats Bear's hand away. Actually, I think it's more that Bear lets him knock it away. "Maybe I am the omen!"

"Calm down, omen-boy," I say. "As long as you can follow directions, we'll all get along."

Rubbing his nose, Damien seethes. "O.K."

Keeping ourselves close to the ground and behind the temporary cover of the chairs, we peek out into the aisles. One or two people remain, wrestling in vain, trying desperately to free themselves. Up on the left, a guy with a ball cap. On the right, a woman with pink-and-blue hair.

"Now . . . Damien," I say, "wait here until I give you the signal it's safe to move." To Bear, "You and Chase free up the guy on the left." I look back over my shoulder at Liza. "You can wait here or help me free the woman."

She shakes her head. "Oh no-no-no. I'll wait right here. Sorry."

"OK—"

There's a whistling sound followed by a thump as an arrow punches through the seat in front of us, the arrowhead stopping just short of my nose. I jump. Liza jumps. Everyone jumps. How these invisible archers managed a shot like that is beyond me, but then again, I'm no marksman myself.

Liza grabs my shoulder, squeezes it so hard I wince. "Never mind. I'm following you."

I nod at her, then to Bear. "Let's go!"

Bear makes his way up front with Chase reluctantly close behind. The two of them slip into the ball-cap guy's aisle and get to work releasing him.

I glance back at Liza. "Keep your head down."

"You don't have to tell me twice!" she replies.

We move into the aisle, creeping along as if inside a dark tunnel. Heads low, the occasional sound of an arrow flying above our head. Pebbles of tempered glass litter the floor. I'm careful where I place my hands and knees to avoid cutting myself. Pangs of fear nip at my insides, sending sharp bursts of heat and adrenaline-fueled quakes through my body. The bus feels as though it's a mile long, but it's not.

It's just the panic distorting everything around me.

We get to the pink-and-blue-haired woman's aisle. She glances down at us and repeatedly nods to the seat next to her where two arrows landed just inches from her head. I yank the tape off her face, she gasps and for a split-second, and I'm caught off guard.

She's beautiful—

"Hurry up!" she barks.

I make quick work of her restraints, cutting with a now very, very dull knife. Within moments, though, she's free. She slides down

27

onto the floor next to us, and a waft of her perfume and hairspray gives my nose a welcome break from the stench of fear and piss.

"Thanks," she says breathlessly. "Pretty sure I was next."

Two arrows zoom above our heads and punch through her seat.

The three of us exchange looks.

"I think we're all next," Liza says, her voice trembling.

"Screw that," I say. "We're getting out of here." I poke my head out into the aisle and Bear does as well. He gives me another thumbs-up. I then call out, "Damien!"

Nothing.

No sign of him.

"DAMIEN!"

Damien finally leans out into the aisle, his shaggy, jet-black hair spilling over his eyes. "What?"

"Get your ass up here!"

"Is that the"—Damien makes quotes with his fingers—"sign?"

"OK, smart-ass. Stay and die."

"Whatever." Damien worms his way up toward us. He slips into the aisle across from us, a frown firmly planted on his eighteen-year-old face.

I'm just guessing his age, but he's at the ripe youthful age of rebellion and suburban anger-for-no-reason. The last thing I'm going to do is feed into his bad attitude when we've got bigger issues.

"So . . . what's the plan, boss?" Bear asks me.

I suddenly freeze. "The plan?"

I feel that unwelcome hand of dread reach up from the pit of my stomach, clutch my vocal chords, and steal my breath. I choke.

What is the plan?

Bear leans close. My fear is reflected in his eyes as he asks once again, "Yeah. What do we do now?"

Good question.

5

It's Your Funeral

"Hold that thought," I tell Bear as I snap out of my anxious stupor. I'm amazed that in a matter of mere minutes these people have adopted me as their leader. I have no clue how we're going to get out of this.

Whatever this is.

Guess I'm going to have to suck it up and roll with the adage: Fake it 'til you make it.

Or more simply: Keep moving, or die panicking.

I climb over Liza, peeking just high enough to look out the window. I do this assuming our invisible assassins are not flying above us or perched atop some trees close by. And rather than being hit by arrows, the first thing to hit me is the faint smell of decay; of something rotting in the distance. The stench is so strong I have to fight the urge to turn away. But I resist. The last thing I want to do is turn my head or close my eyes and give our assailants the chance to off me.

Centered in the sky hangs a full moon, fat, and milky-white. Surrounding it, an expanse of stars sparkle like a million pieces of broken glass. I've never gazed up at such a perfect display of the cosmos. It's brighter than I ever would have pictured. The crisp radiance of these celestial bodies, unobscured by the haze of smog or man-made light. The type of night sky that a stargazer would appreciate. It's also the kind of starlight you get when you're many miles away from the nearest major city.

I then catch sight of something else—a bizarre red mist that carpets the ground. It's as if a fog machine were pumping out exhaust from Hell. Thanks to the unusual light source, I make out that we're in the middle of a field full of gnarly weeds and tall grass. Roughly a football field away, a bank of trees encircles us, also backlit by the same soft, red lighting illuminating the fog.

So where the heck is that light coming from?

A gray shadow darts through the landscape then dives into the grass. Followed by another, emerging from the wall of trees to the right. It too vanishes into the sea of weeds and twisted shrubbery.

"Great," I say under my breath.

"What?" Liza asks, her words coming out quick. "What-is-it? What? Tell us!"

I duck back down, flip around to face her and the rest of the group. All eyes on me. All eyes expecting bad news.

"Well, we're definitely not alone," I say.

"No shit, Sherlock," Damien snaps.

I ignore him. "And there's more than one of them—whoever they are."

"More than one of who?" Chase's voice cracks like a thirteen-year-old going through puberty. "Who the fuck is out there? And what do they want—?"

"It doesn't matter," Bear says, his tone unwavering, almost calm. "Clearly they just want us dead." I'm sort of jealous of his cool demeanor. Maybe he should lead the group.

"Oh well, that's just perfect." Chase turns to me. "So what do we do?"

He's asking me.

Maybe me giving up the lead isn't such a bright idea?

Maybe they're looking up to me since I freed them?

Maybe—

"Well?" Chase asks, snapping his fingers in front of my face. "What do we do?"

I shake off the spiraling doubt. Lock eyes with Chase. "Well, we can't stay here."

"Why not?" The dude with the ball cap finally speaks up. Everyone turns to him. He raises his hand tepidly as he says, "I'm . . . Aaron by the way."

Damien rolls his eyes.

"And thanks..." Aaron says as he clears his throat, "for saving me."

Bear nods.

"We can't stay here because whoever is out there is on the move," I say. "Looks like they're headed toward us. Clearly, the bus isn't safe."

"Any of you geniuses think about just driving us off into the sunset?" Damien asks. "Maybe the keys are up front."

The woman with the pink-and-blue hair crawls toward the front of the bus and then crawls back. "My first thought, too," she says. "But they tore the crap out of the steering column." She shrugs. "And then they took the steering wheel."

"Well, that's just great!" Chase shouts. "That's just . . . fucking . . . great—"

"Calm down, son." Bear places one of his massive lumberjack hands on Chase's shoulder and squeezes so hard Chase cowers, flinching in pain. "Things could be worse."

"Oh really?" Chase's tone again climbs an octave as he asks, "Like how?"

"I dunno. Ask him." Bear nods toward one of the passengers, one whose throat is skewed by an arrow.

Chase shakes off Bear's grip, pouting.

"All right, then," Aaron says to me. "So what do you propose we do?"

"Just a guess," I say, "but looks like we've got about a hundred yards of open field between us and a dense bank of trees off to our left. I say we make a run for them."

Damien scoffs. Shakes his head as if what I said was funny.

31

I glare at him. "Better than just sitting here waiting for Lord knows what."

"I think I'd rather wait here," Aaron says.

The lights in the cabin go out.

Liza whimpers.

A squeal escapes Chase.

"There goes the battery," the woman with the pink-and-blue hair says as she looks up at the ceiling.

"Still want to stay here?" Bear asks Aaron.

"Actually, yeah, I kind of do."

As my eyes adjust to the darkness, which is somewhat illuminated by the red glow outside, I notice everyone is staring at Aaron as if he just said something insane.

"Look, you're suggesting that we run out there. Expose ourselves to our killers." Aaron takes off his ball cap and uses it to wipe the sweat from his brow. "I'd rather hunker down here. Wait until first light. Then make a move."

"And what if whatever's out there doesn't want to wait until first light?" I ask. "What if whatever's out there wants to kill you first, and then watch the sun rise?"

Aaron firmly plants his ball cap back on his head. "I'll take my chances."

"Fine." I lean into the aisle so I can see everyone's faces a little more clearly. "Anyone else wants to stay?"

"I sorta do," Liza says, sniffling as she speaks. "I'm not much of a runner."

"Neither am I. I'm a smoker. I'm sure I've got the lungs of a coal miner," Bear says. "But I'm not going to sit and wait for anyone to make a shish kebab outta me."

"I think they're insane for going," Aaron tells Liza. "I say stay with me if you want to live through this."

Liza exchanges glances between Aaron and me.

After a few beats, she says, "I'm staying," a sense of impending breakdown in her voice.

My instincts scream to me that it's a death sentence for the two of them.

"Are you sure?" I ask.

She nods her head, but even under the dim light from the red haze spilling in from outside, I catch a hint of uncertainty in her eyes.

There's a scream from outside. We all jump.

The scream is ugly.

Unearthly.

It sounds human . . . but not.

It's more of a shriek. A scream from the top of something's lungs.

Or maybe even someone's.

"Jesus, what was that?" Chase's gaze shifts between all of us, searching for answers as if we know any better ourselves.

It happens again.

Another scream. This one is a little deeper. And more like a yodel.

No. Not a yodel.

A war cry.

It's a freaking war cry!

This is the stuff of movies. Ones featuring armies of natives, chanting and bellowing in tongues never heard before by modern man.

Only this is no movie.

This time something big sails into the cabin, embedding itself into the back wall of the bus.

We all turn our heads to see a spear—a goddamn spear—jutting out from the back wall.

"Alrighty! That's our cue," I say. "Who's coming with me?"

"OK, seriously," Chase says, "maybe Aaron is right about staying, man. I mean, whatever the hell's out there is taunting us. Maybe they want us to come outside."

He could be right.

Actually, he probably is right.

But the alternative is to sit here and wait for them to climb onboard and kill us where we crouch.

"I'm willing to take that chance," I say as I push past everyone and crawl toward the back of the bus. I hop up to my feet and pull as hard as I can, yanking the spear free from the wall. I drop to the floor just as an arrow cruises above my head, landing right where I was seconds before.

Yep.

They're watching us all right.

And so is everyone on this bus. Watching me with awe as I crawl back toward them.

Not long before this nightmare, I almost put a bullet in my brain. Of my own free will. If I'm at the point of considering killing myself, I'd say that makes me liberated enough to take some chances. Maybe do something worthy with my life instead of sulking, or taking selfish action against myself.

I feel like such a faker right now. A coward. How could these people, these strangers, be putting their faith in a man who nearly buried a bullet in the back of his skull?

Fake it 'til you make it, Rodney.

Keep moving or die panicking.

Those two thoughts send a sudden surge of confidence through me. What have I got to lose now? I've already lost everything that ever mattered to me. If this is my new rock bottom, screw dying on someone—or something—else's terms!

I slide up next to the group and lift the end of the spear to their faces. Their attention on the blade tip and then me.

"I'll be damned if I'm going to sit here and let these pricks cherry-pick us. Nor am I gonna play their little game. Nor, for that matter, Jim Grimm's game. I'd rather go out there and die trying." I survey everyone's eyes. The tinge of red light reflecting on them. I need to know who is with me. "Now . . . if any of you want to join me, speak up, raise a hand right now. Otherwise, this is where we part ways."

A moment of shared silence.

A moment of deep, internal deliberation.

Bear, Chase, and the woman with the pink-and-blue hair slowly raise their hands.

"I'm still staying," Aaron says flatly, seemingly unconvinced by any of the obvious reasons—in my humble opinion—to get the heck off the bus.

Liza avoids my gaze, tears brimming and sliding down her cheeks. "Sorry," she says as she shrinks away. "I ain't cut out for all that running around. I'll wait it out here. The Lord's got my back."

"Well maybe the Lord sent me!" I shout, not even sure of what I'm saying.

Liza doesn't flinch.

Dammit! It's a death sentence. It sucks, but I can't force her to go. Then again, I can't guarantee everyone's safety once we are outside, either. Still, it's a risk I'm 100 percent willing to take.

I look to Damien.

"I don't know yet, man," he says with a yawn.

I glare at the little punk, recalling kids like him back in high school. They were the bullies. They were the against-the-grain, anti-culture rebels without a clue. And this kid definitely has no clue. Part of that teenage immortality belief that we've all shared at some point in our youth. A belief that quickly evaporates when death bitch-slaps you in the face. When you lose someone close to you.

Or when you consider eating a bullet yourself.

I shrug Damien off. To the others, I ask, "You guys ready?"

"Hold up. I said I'm not sure yet," Damien says. "I didn't say no."

"Cut the crap, emo boy!" Bear grabs Damien, brings him so close their noses touch. "In case you haven't been keeping score here we're down by six. Either you're coming with us, or you're taking your chances here with these two. It's that simple."

"Get off me, tubs." Damien pushes Bear away from him. "And thanks for helping me make up my mind. The last thing I want to do is tag along with you faggots."

"Fine. It's your funeral," I say.

"Yeah-yeah-yeah. Cool," he says without blinking.

Such a weirdo. There's just so much wrong about Damien. Like why is he so nonchalant given the situation? Like why—

No time to psychoanalyze this jerk. The others are looking to me.

"Let's move." I turn toward the front of the bus, crawling as quickly as possible, dragging the spear alongside me. Chase, Bear, and the woman with pink-and-blue hair follow close behind.

"Yo, Rodney!" Damien yells. "It's Rodney, right?"

I glance over my shoulder.

A wicked smile spreads across his lips and under the red glow cast from outside he almost looks like a devil. "Be saying a prayer for ya," he says with a wink.

The comment catches me off guard.

The kid is baked.

"I'm pretty sure you don't pray," I say as I grab the door handle. I take a deep breath.

Here we go.

6

The Bus Stop

"Ready?" I ask.

Bear and woman with the pink-and-blue hair nod.

However, Chase just gapes at me with that same slack-jawed, deer-in-the-headlights look he's had on his face since I freed him from his seat. I share the sentiment, but thankfully I'm suppressing it . . . somehow. Fear is taking a temporary backseat to the desire to escape this massacre.

"Chase . . . are you ready?" I ask.

A beat, then, "Yeah-yeah-yeah." He wipes away the fresh sheen of sweat on his face.

I give him a quick pat on the shoulder. A reassuring gesture, perhaps for both of us. There's a chance that I could be completely wrong. We could totally go out there and get ourselves slaughtered. Then Damien would have the satisfaction of telling Liza and Aaron he was glad he didn't go with us.

But then again, it wasn't me who threw us into this real-life manhunt.

It was Jim Grimm—or whoever he's working with. Whoever it is that is placing bets, or managing this sick game.

"All right, guys. On three. Follow me, drop to the ground, and stay close to the bus." As I speak, I get a distinct feeling that they're half-listening, half-thinking about what getting a spear to the chest might feel like. "No doubt they'll take aim as soon as we exit, so be ready to dive into that grass like it's a damn swimming pool."

Bear nods. So does the woman with the pink-and-blue hair. Chase remains frozen. As if someone hit his pause button. "Chase!"

"Yeah?"

"Did you hear me?"

"Y-y-yeah." If Chase doesn't get a hold of his nerves, he's going to do himself in.

"Are you listening?"

"Yes! I'm listening." Chase grabs both sides of his head as if it is about to explode. "Jesus Christ!" he lets out with a gasp. "I'm just a little freaked out, people, in case you haven't noticed!"

"Oh, we noticed," Bear says under his breath.

"Ha! What a pussy!" Damien cackles from the rear of the bus. "He's scared. I bet he shit his pants."

Chase turns back to him, spraying spittle as he shouts, "Fuck off and go get a real haircut, emo boy!"

"Yeah, I'll get right on that," Damien says with a chuckle.

I grab Chase, force him to look at me. "We're all scared. But if we stay, we die." The worried expression on his face doesn't change. "Still not convinced? Why don't you ask the other passengers on this bus?"

"Hey, thanks for the vote of confidence," I hear Aaron say. "Assholes."

"All right-all right-all right." Chase shrugs me off as if I'm his fight doctor and now he's finally ready to get in the ring. "I got it. I got it. We're screwed no matter what. So let's just do this."

"Wonderful," the woman with the pink-and-blue hair says with a huff. "Let's go already. All of this debating isn't helping the situation get any better."

"Agreed," I say with a nod. I take another deep breath. "Ready?" I look to each one in the group. Double-checking that they are still onboard. Tiny sparkles of sweat gather on the woman with the pink-

38

and-blue hair's forehead, and I realize it is true what they say.

Men sweat. Women glow.

There's definitely a radiance about her, but it's caused by something beyond her looks. There's this energy she seems to exude. Something different. Like there's more to her story. And I don't even know her name. Here I was giving Damien crap, and I didn't bother to even ask her for her name—

Damien snaps me out of my thoughts with, "Good luck, retards!"

"OK, guys." Ignoring Damien, I tell the group, "On three."

Whatever is waiting for us out there might have been waiting for this moment.

The moment we all decide to abandon ship. The moment we enter their world. The moment we expose ourselves to their game. But then again, that's already happened.

The minute we got on this godforsaken bus.

"One."

Chase closes his eyes. Takes several quick breaths as if he's going to go underwater.

"Two."

Bear takes one deep breath himself. His barrel chest swelling as he gulps in the fetid air around us.

"Three!"

I pull on the door handle and nearly trip over the steps on my way down. The ground comes up quick. I land with a thud, kicking up sand in my wake. The spear slips out of my hand.

Great!

Adding to the symphony of crickets outside, I hear everyone stumble, and spill out all around me. This is going a lot clumsier than I had thought. At least we have some semblance of cover within the tall grass surrounding the bus.

There's a blur of motion. I feel arms and legs everywhere, hitting me in the face, the ribs, my backside. I taste grass and dirt. Our exit from the bus unfolds more like an end-zone tackle than a smooth escape.

Someone yells out, "Holy shit!"

There's a grunt.

Someone lands on me and knocks the wind out of me.

Thankfully that someone is light. And they smell kind of . . . pleasant?

Well, anything right now is better than the smell of piss and panic.

I roll over, we meet face-to-face—the woman with the pink-and-blue hair. Time stops. I feel her panicked breath brush against my skin. Her hair spills around her cheeks.

For a millisecond, I have a random thought: Her weight feels good on me.

Haven't been this close to a woman in a while.

What a stupid thought in the middle of—

The crickets surrounding us stop chirping.

I get this sensation in my gut, and it's not my libido stirring.

It's dread.

In a flash, a word escapes me: "Move!" I roll her off me just as a volley of arrows showers the bus door.

Someone screams. I think it's Chase.

No—it's not a scream, it's a high-pitched whooping. A bizarre cheering of excitement. Like a hunting party thrilled that they're close to catching their prey.

It's that war cry again.

"Everyone! Under the bus!" I shout. As I shift my body around, my leg kicks something—the spear. I grab it and wriggle my way under the bus. I glance to either side and catch Bear, Chase, and the woman with the pink-and-blue hair crawling up next to me. We're all panting, breathless. A mixture of terror and adrenaline coursing through our bodies. The full moon above, along with the eerie red glow, casts just enough light on everyone's faces that I can still discern who's who.

"Now what?" Bear asks me, catching his breath.

Yeah, Rodney.

Now what?

Before I can think, let alone answer, someone peers under the bus and lets out this unearthly wail—the earsplitting sound of someone or something either in a lot of pain . . . or about to inflict pain themselves. I feel every single hair on my body stand on end.

"What the fuck!" Chase squeals.

The red haze outlines the figure in enough detail for me to make out a muscular man with the ripped physique of a CrossFit athlete. His screaming subsides, but his mouth still hangs open. Serrated, bright-white teeth glimmer under the moonlight like a row of iridescent candles. His eyes ignite; two hot coals burning bright shades of orange, yellow, and red.

His natural display of supernatural special effects sends a quiver of fear through my stomach. My body locks up. I'm overcome with panic.

The gasps and moans tell me that fear is overwhelming all of us.

The man's fiery eyes twitch erratically as he studies the group. His gaze hungry, sizing up each one of us as if we are entrée choices in a buffet line and he isn't sure where to start. He abruptly lets out another horrifying, deafening screech, and brandishes some sort of primitive hammer.

But before he can strike, the will to live exceeds my fear, and I raise my spear and drive it into his chest. His mouth opens impossibly wide as he lets out a shriek that could crack glass. Blood sprays my face, gets into my eyes. It smells like rotten meat.

Smells putrid.

Spoiled.

Dead.

He shrinks away, taking the spear with him, hands clutching it futilely. He staggers backward, trips and lands flat on his back. He shudders for a few seconds and then stops moving altogether. The spear sticks up from his body like a morbid flagpole.

"Who was that?" Chase shouts.

I look at Chase, then at the body, then at Chase again. Between panicked breaths, I say, "No . . . idea." As I wipe the blood from my face, another war cry erupts in the distance. "But clearly he's got friends."

Bear pushes past us, toward the dead man.

"What are you doing?" the woman with the pink-and-blue hair asks. There's a tremble in her tone that we all share.

Bear tells her to hush. Reaches for something. Lifts up the man's weapon. From what we know, it's a stick with a rock tied to the end of it. As he crawls back, he says, "It's some sort of . . . tomahawk."

"Seriously! What's going on?" Chase asks.

"Isn't it obvious?" I ask. "We're being hunted."

7

One of You

I motion for everyone to come close. They do, writhing together into a tight bundle. There's very little clearance with the bus above our heads, but at least that leaves us with only four distinct directions we must monitor for movement.

"What do you mean we're being hunted?" Chase asks me as he brushes his forearm across his face, wiping away the sweat that's accumulated within the last few moments.

"I mean, we're being hunted."

Bear then asks Chase, "Did you miss that asshole's monologue back on the bus?"

"Of course not!" Chase snarls, his teeth appearing a pinkish-white under the ambient glow. "Was I having a panic attack? Sure was. Difficult to focus on someone's speech when you're too busy freaking out about being strapped to a goddamn seat—"

"Shut up, already!" The woman with the pink-and-blue hair covers Chase's mouth with her hand. Looking to me, she asks, "So why this game? What's the point?"

"For fun? For shits and giggles? For money? Who knows?" I say. "All that matters is we're going to find a way out of this."

A flare goes off to the east, racing upward into the sky, sparkling brighter as it climbs, then it sails downward, fading behind the wall of trees.

43

Chase swats the woman's hand away. "What was that?"

"That's where they want us to go," I answer as the bitter taste of stomach acid—a result of the roiling dread in my stomach—stings the back of my throat.

"And how do you know that?" Chase asks.

"You really didn't listen, did you?" Bear shakes his head.

"OK, no! I didn't!"

"I know that because that's what Jim mentioned," I explain. "He said a flare would mark the safe zone."

"But why direct us to a safe zone?" the woman asks.

"Because they don't want us to just sit on the bus and get picked off. They want us to play." I take a deep breath, then add, "Wouldn't be much of a game if we just sat around and waited to die, now would it?"

"No, it wouldn't," she answers.

Bear pounds the tomahawk into the ground and says, "Guess we'll just have to change the game."

"Oh great. Beautiful." Chase wipes the sweat off his face again, this time with his entire hand. It does little to dry him. "So basically what you guys are suggesting is that we follow the light? Go where they want us to go?"

I nod. "In the direction I initially said we should go. Toward that bank of trees to the east."

"So, what? So that they can jump us?" Chase asks.

"They've already jumped us, dumbass!" the woman with the pink-and-blue hair snaps.

Another war cry—this one closer.

"OK, enough planning," I say. "Let's get moving—"

"Oh, no-no-no-no-no! I'm not going out there. Screw that!" Chase worms away from us. "I'm getting back on the bus, that's what I'm doing. I don't care if I have to wait until morning, I'm not—"

Another war cry cuts through the night.

This cry is only several feet away from us.

Bear rolls his massive body toward Chase, wraps one arm around him then puts a single finger on Chase's lips, gesturing for him to shut up.

A patch of the tall grass in front of us stirs. Another one of those men rises, like a prairie dog emerging from its hole. He approaches the fallen body of his comrade, places his hand on the spear, and with one swift motion, pulls it out. Raising it above his head, he cries out.

"MWAHHHH!" he roars. "MWAAAAAAAAAAAAAH!"

It's a booming call. One that makes my skin crawl. It's an exclamation of anger, furor, and sadness. Well, it's hard to say for sure how many layered emotions there are bundled into the man's unearthly shrieks.

I can hear Chase's muffled cries, and the mixed breaths of fear from everyone else, as we watch the man pump the spear in the air. Under the glint of the moonlight and the blanketing red haze surrounding us, his skin appears pinkish-gray. Ashen like that of a corpse. He's bald except for a thick tangle of hair running down the center of the crown of his scalp. Several feathers protrude from behind his head. He's either dressed like a Native American as part of this sick hunting game. Or he really is one.

His eyes suddenly flicker to life as if sparklers were set off inside his irises. They alternate shades of red and orange and yellow. He bellows out another war cry, exposing rows of jagged, luminescent teeth—

He stops screaming. Head snapping in our direction.

My first thought: he sees us, huddled together under the bus chassis, shrouded by the shadows.

Wait.

It's not us he's looking at.

He's looking inside the bus.

Aaron, Liza, and Damien must've seen him, too, because we hear a flurry of footsteps and muted conversations right above our heads. This is followed by Aaron shouting, "Move, move, move," and, "Get over there," followed by, "Get down, get down, get down."

But it's not like they're on a cruise ship.

They're trapped on a bus.

There aren't many places to go or hide.

The hunter leaps with superhuman strength onto the roof of the bus. We roll onto our backs, listening intently. The metal roof groans with each of the hunter's steps.

Aaron belts out more commands. More of the same. But there's nowhere to go. They're trapped. Mice in a cage. Yet we hear them move about. Footfalls thumping against the floor of the bus as they try in vain to find that safe spot—

Glass shatters.

Someone screams.

"No, no, no, noooooooo!" Aaron shouts. "Oh God, please! Please!"

Chase struggles to breathe, air whistling as it escapes between Bear's fingers. Bear's massive hand nearly covers Chase's entire face, suppressing his protests rather efficiently.

"Shhhh!" Bear says.

"PLEEEEEEEEEAAAAAAAAAASE!" Aaron pleads.

This is followed by a loud gurgling sound.

Like someone vomiting.

Or being cut open.

Our gazes fixed on the underside of the bus, we trace the sounds of footsteps with our eyes. Hefty steps that make their way toward the back of the bus. Toward Damien or Liza.

"We should leave," I whisper to the others. "Now. While that man—that thing—is distracted."

"You mean leave them behind?" the woman with the pink-and-blue hair asks.

"They wanted to stay, remember?" I slide out of from under the bus, into the sea of grass ahead. Keeping low to the ground, I turn back to them and signal for them to follow. "Come on. Let's go!"

There's a moment of hesitation. Then everyone files out.

"Stay close," I tell them.

"What now?" Chase asks.

I point east. "Now we make our way to those trees."

"That's a long way to crawl, man," Chase says. "Those trees are like a mile away."

"Who said we're going to crawl the whole way?"

Bear shoots me a look.

"First we crawl. Then we run," I say this with such confidence, I surprise myself. Maybe all those years managing shitty people for my shitty boss actually taught me something about being a leader.

Hopefully not a shitty leader.

"Now," I say, feeling my own breathing pick up. Adrenaline starting to flow. I hope I'm not making a mistake, but I continue anyway. "When I tell you guys to run, you run! Got it?"

Everyone nods.

"OK, let's go."

We make our way into the thick grass using the moon as a guide. The red glow on the ground brightens.

"What's with the special effects?" Chase asks, his voice barely a whisper.

"The what?" Bear asks.

"The red lights?"

"I don't know," Bear says. "Want to go back and ask?"

"Not really."

"Then shut up and keep moving."

"My sentiments exactly," the woman says.

We crawl away from the bus as quickly as possible. Behind us, we hear Damien crying out, not in pain.

But in protest.

"I'm one of you, you stupid dipshits!" His voice rises to a pitch that could probably be heard from miles around. "What are you doing? Aren't you listening? I'm one of you!"

The urge to peek above the grass and look back at the bus is tempting,

47

but my gut screams at me to keep moving, which is exactly what I tell everyone to do.

"I'M ONE OF YOU!" Damien's pleas are so loud, they cover any noises we're making. We pick up the pace.

"I'M ONE OF YOU!"

We continue slinking our way through the ocean of grass and weeds and wet patches of ground. As Damien's cries fade behind us, I figure this is as good a time as any . . .

To make a run for it.

"OK, guys!" I jump to my feet. "Run!"

"What?" Chase asks.

Bear clutches Chase by the shirt. "He said run!"

Everyone hops up and makes for the wall of trees.

Damien stops shouting.

A cold, dead silence follows.

A vacuum of sound.

Even the crickets remain quiet.

There's just the noise of the four of us gasping, wheezing, and crushing grass in our wake as we haul ass. But the steady thump-thump-thump of our feet hitting the ground is soon drowned out by the encroaching war cries . . .

Of more hunters on the way.

8

The Name Game

We're running faster than I've ever run in my life. Difficult to tell if we're being followed. I can't distinguish the racket we're making from the distant sounds of the hunters' cries from somewhere around us.

My lungs take in the damp, humid air. The fiery burn of lactic acid stings the insides of my calves and hamstrings. I half expect at any point that one of us is going to take an arrow or spear to the back. This expectation sends a spur of dread that prickles down my spine.

However, instead of any of us falling prey to primitive weapons, we safely make it to the wall of trees. Instinctively all of us dive down to the ground as if going for a touchdown. As if we've reached some sort of safety zone.

After a moment's rest, everyone slowly sits up, chests heaving, gasping for air. My heart feels as though it's about to explode. Lungs gasping desperately for precious oxygen. The effects of my sympathetic nervous system piloting my body on overdrive. Blood is pumping so violently through my body, I can feel my heartbeat in my ears.

"We . . . we made it!" Chase says. "We freaking made it!"

"Made it?" the woman with the pink-and-blue hair asks, her shoulders rising and falling with each breath. "We're still in the middle of nowhere!"

Several bright, yellow flares sail through the air, arcing downward. They land on the roof of the bus.

"Look!" Bear is breathing so hard he can barely get the words out. "More . . . flares."

More flares?

Wait.

No.

Those aren't flares.

They're arrows

Flaming arrows to be exact. Dozens more of them rain down on the bus. Their fire-tipped ends embedding themselves into nearly every square foot of the bus's exterior. Within a matter of seconds, the entire vehicle is ablaze.

"Well, thank God we didn't stay there!" Chase says, and I can't help but shoot him a dirty look.

"Come on," I say, getting to my feet. "We got to keep going."

"Where?" Chase throws up his arms.

"Toward that first flare. Are you deaf?"

"No, I'm just not dumb." Chase clears his throat as if to make a point. "I'm still not 100 percent convinced that this flare bullshit is really going to end all that well for us."

"All right. That's it." Bear hops to his feet, picks Chase off the ground and pins him to a tree. "I'm a little sick of your attitude—"

"Let go!"

"And that sickness is amplified by the fact that you're a city boy." Bear leans in close. "That's two strikes against you."

"You're hurting me!"

"If I hurt you, you wouldn't be talking." Bear lightly smacks Chase's cheek. "Now I don't know about you, but I'm going to make it out of this alive. I didn't get out of prison only to turn around and die in the middle of a goddamn field!" Bear shakes him. "Now pull that stick from out your ass and calm down, capiche?"

Chase is motionless. Mouth wide open, he looks like he wants to scream but doesn't. Instead, he squeaks out, "Capiche."

Bear releases Chase, who drops to the ground like a bag of bricks.

"Look . . ." Chase rubs his neck, straightens his collar as he gets to his feet. "I'm just a little freaked out, OK?"

"A little freaked?" Bear asks.

Chase dusts himself off. "OK, so scared shitless is more accurate!"

Ignoring Chase's antics, the woman with the pink-and-blue hair asks Bear, "So what'd you go to prison for?"

Bear pauses. Chooses his words carefully. "Being stupid."

"Oh, because smart people end up in prison," she says.

Bear shoots her a cross look.

She gets to her feet. "No, really. What'd you do?"

"I'll tell you if you tell us your name."

"I don't like my name."

"I don't like what I did," Bear answers.

"Which was?" she presses.

"I helped commit a robbery. Things went south. An innocent woman got shot." Bear glances at the ground briefly, then back to her. "That's all you need to know."

The woman studies him as if trying to get a read on him, but Bear's about as expressive as a rock. Finally, she says, "My name's Kylie."

"Ha!" Chase chuckles to himself. "I thought you were going to say something like Gertrude, Maribel, or Betty Anne. Kylie's not such a bad name."

"It's my mother's name." Kylie's eyes burn into him. It's a piercing gaze that could cut glass. I'm glad I'm not on the receiving end. Chase shrinks.

"What's so bad about that?" Bear asks.

"My mother was a bitch," she says. "Couldn't really handle the fact that I was . . . different than my brothers and sisters."

"Different?"

Kylie closes her eyes, seemingly suppressing some nuclear emotion going off inside her. "Let's save the therapy session for later, OK, guys? You know my name. Congratulations." She reopens her eyes and nods back toward the burning bus. "Now we should get our asses moving. Those freaks are not that far behind us."

"That's assuming they know we left," Chase adds.

"Well then let's assume that," I say.

It's as if they heard our conversation because another flare flies upward to the east. It brightens the sky momentarily like a falling star only at close range. A shroud of white light encircles it as it reaches its zenith, then arcs downward.

"You guys think they can hear us or something?" Kylie asks.

"Maybe. Maybe not." As I watch the flare disappear deep into the forest, it hits me. "Or maybe they've been taking attendance."

"What do you mean?" Kylie asks.

"Maybe they've kept track of who left the bus, and they know that four passengers are missing," I say, feeling the dread build up inside me once more. "This is their game after all. It only makes sense that they would've shot the flares off. They wouldn't have done that if they knew we were all slaughtered back on the bus."

"They could've just assumed and shot the flare off anyway," Kylie says.

"They could've, but I doubt it," I tell her this though I'm not even sure how I'm so confident of this myself.

Something is watching us.

Something is tracking our movements.

Maybe it's the hunters. Or maybe it's someone else.

"So, what should we do?" Bear asks as he peers off in the direction of the flare. "Do you think we should—"

"Wait-wait-wait a second!" Chase waves his hands in the air, cuts between us. "Why are you guys asking him? Who nominated Rodney team captain?"

"Last I checked"—Bear leans close to Chase—"if it weren't for him, we would've either been skewered or barbecued on that bus. I'll gladly follow him wherever he goes." With that, he shoves Chase so hard he nearly knocks him over. "Meantime, if you've got a better idea, knock yourself out, amigo. No one's going to stop you, that's for sure."

Chase straightens his shirt. Lets out a grumble. "Whatever."

"Anyway..." Bear clears his throat, then asks me once again, "The plan?"

"Well, like you said before, we're going to show them how our version of the game is going to be played." I watch the last bit of light from the flare fizzle in the distance. "We're going to keep playing until we win. We're going to the source of that flare, and we're going to kick their ass." I nod. "Now let's move!"

9

A Surprise Visitor

The ambient glow permeating the woods gave us more than enough light to avoid running into trees and clusters of shrubbery. The thick mist blankets the ground, brightened by a red light. It's as if a network of LED lights has been woven into the soil, illuminating every step. There's no simple explanation for where this light is emanating from, but I'm grateful for it. Without it, we'd be navigating this jungle in nearly pitch-black conditions with only the occasional flash of moonlight breaking between openings in the treetops.

As we make our way through the dense forest, the tree trunks seem to close in around us as if we're wading through a crowd of shadows at a rock concert. Twigs and leaves snap under our feet, the soft dirt giving way with each step. The ground is uneven, and one wrong step could reward one of us with a twisted ankle—a serious inconvenience. The pungent smell of smoke coming from the bus permeates the woods, serving as a reminder that our pursuers are still very much on our tails.

That whoever those men are, they're no doubt coming after us.

I glance over my shoulder, making sure that I'm not running by myself. The sound of my own breathing and my legs pounding into the ground with each clumsy step is deafening in and of itself.

Thankfully the group is keeping up with me.

Kylie is right at my side. Chase, clearly not the athlete, stumbles clumsily over the terrain. Bear trails us, his hulking frame slowing him down. He's panting so hard, I worry he might pass out.

I come to a stop, and everyone hits their brakes. Bear leans over, hands propped on his knees, heaving, gasping for air. He looks up at us, and under the haze of the red mist, I see that he's sweating profusely. Perhaps more so than the rest of us.

"I'm an ex-smoker," he says between wheezing, pained breaths. "But not ex enough."

Then again, we're all gasping for air. Seems that this momentary break is just enough for our nerves and our bodies to catch up with our situation.

A war cry cuts through the woods like an arrow itself. We all straighten up. Eyes and heads darting everywhere.

"Jesus, that sounded close!" Chase says as he spins around, scanning for any signs of movement.

"Yeah, it did," Kylie says.

"Shh!" I say, putting a finger to my lips.

Another war cry—this one even closer.

"Everybody, get down." I lower myself to the ground and gesture to the others to do the same. There's a rotting log a few feet away. We plant ourselves behind it and turn our gaze back toward the bus in the distance. It sparkles like a tiny orange gem.

"Shouldn't we be running?" Chase whispers.

I feel everyone's eyes on me, no doubt wondering the same thing. "Well?"

I turn to Chase. "Shhhhhhhhhhhh..."

A deathly stillness follows. Nothing stirs. No bats or birds fly by. There's no breeze. Heck, even the crickets are quiet.

"Rodney, seriously," Chase whispers. "What are we waiting for—?"

Bear smacks him on the back of the head.

Chase winces, lowers his head like a scolded toddler, then mutters, "Jerk," under his breath.

Silence follows. Feels like an eternity before we hear something.

Straight ahead, a twig snaps. A shadow dashes between the trees.

Oh crap.

It's another one of those hunters.

As he makes his way toward us, I get a glimpse of the hunter's sculpted frame. Feathers protruding from the top of his head, flopping like an antenna as he hops over fallen trees and tall patches of grass with the effortless agility of a panther. His silhouette outlined by the moon, backlit by the red fog all around. For all we know, he could be the Devil himself.

And the Devil is coming straight toward us.

"You think he knows we're here?" Chase asks, his whisper almost loud enough for the hunter to hear.

"I don't know," I whisper.

The hunter closes in. The thumping of his footfalls grows louder by the second.

Bear brings his tomahawk up near his face, clutching it tightly. I wish I still had a weapon myself. All I have is the tiny blade on my pocket knife.

The footfalls draw near. The hunters are almost upon us when he disappears behind a cluster of tall pines.

Silence engulfs the night once more.

For a moment, the only noises I hear are the sounds of everyone's breathing. Fear in each exhalation. Then we hear more footsteps from off in the distance.

"Jeeeee-sus," Chase says. "Sounds like there's a herd of those things headed our way." He starts to get up, but I yank him back down. He turns to me, eyes milky white and full of dread.

"Stay. Put," I tell Chase, bringing my face close to his. Chase nods. Something tells me he must've been a handful as a kid.

Just a wild guess.

The second set of footfalls grows louder. Clumsier. More of a drunken stagger than the agile approach of a seasoned predator. Definitely not as coordinated and deft as the other hunter who is headed our way. This one trips several times as he makes his way toward us, but as he draws closer, a swath of moonlight rains down on his face—

Or her face, rather.

This is not just some random female hunter.

It's Liza.

And somehow, she escaped the bus.

Alive?

10

He's Coming for You

"O Lord, please!" Liza howls out as she stumbles through the woods. "Please, help me. Give me your favor, o Lord!"

Liza is nearing the point where one of those hunters disappeared.

Bear smacks my arm. "What do you want to do?"

I turn to him. "I want to help her."

All of us jump to our feet, yell out, "Liza!"

Liza looks in our direction.

"Over here!" We shout this knowing full well any unseen attackers will know our position, but we can't leave her out here to die.

"Aw, Jesus. Thank you, Lord!" she says as she heads right at us.

The hunter who disappeared before Liza arrived emerges out of nowhere. He swings a tomahawk right into her stomach. She doubles over, lets out a horrified yelp.

Bear charges the hunter, who turns to face him just as Bear cracks him across the face with his own commandeered tomahawk. There's a loud thwap! The hunter drops like a cinder block. Bear follows through with a kick to the face, knocking the hunter backward onto the ground.

I rush to Liza's side. "You OK?"

"I'm . . ." She struggles to speak. "I'm . . . all right."

I kneel next to her. She's bleeding from the mouth. There's blood all over her blouse . . . and something protruding from her side.

The broken end of what appears to be an arrow.

"Oh my God," Kylie gasps, covering her mouth with her hands in shock.

"It's . . . all right." Liza's speech is sloppy. She's got the slur of a drunk. "I'm gonna be . . . all right."

Liza faints, nearly falls, but Kylie and I grab her in time. We sit her down next to a tree, resting her back against the tree trunk. Her eyes roll forward as she comes to.

"We're going to get you out of here, OK?" I say.

Liza nods half-heartedly.

"Yeah, Liza, we promise—" Bear barely gets the words out as he cries out in pain.

The hunter is standing behind him, tomahawk in hand.

Luckily he missed Bear's head, but he struck his backside instead.

Bear counters, spinning on his heels. He brings the tomahawk around in a wide arc. Puts all his two hundred-plus pounds into the swing. Connects with the hunter's jaw, sending him spiraling downward onto his back.

Bear straddles him. Pins the hunter to the ground with one hand. Raises the tomahawk above his head with the other hand—

The hunter mumbles something through his bloodied, toothless grin.

"What's that, asshole?" Bear says. "Can't hear you." He releases his grip enough so that the hunter can speak, yet the words coming out of his mouth are completely foreign.

"Chek-tah. Chek-tah," he chants. Hissing out the word as if it were poison to speak. "Chek-taaaaaah!"

"Chek-tah? Well, chek-tah this!" Bear brings down his tomahawk. There's a crack. Blood spatters all over his face. It's as if he crushed a watermelon with the tomahawk.

Chase turns his head, winces.

Bear rolls off the dead hunter, seizes the man's tomahawk, and tosses it over to me.

As I catch it, I ask, "You all right?"

He shoots me an empty look, then glances down at his hands. They're shaking. The shock of our situation has seemingly hit him. "I . . . just need . . . a minute."

"It hurts," Liza cuts in, her voice hoarse. "It really hurts."

Kylie lifts Liza's blouse just enough to get a closer look at the wound. There's enough light to tell that she's bleeding out and won't survive if we don't get her to a hospital soon.

"Just stay with us, OK, sweetheart?" Kylie rubs Liza's shoulders. Wipes the sweat from the woman's brow.

"How'd you manage to get away?" Chase asks Liza.

"What?" Liza's eyes flutter, head bobbing up and down. She's about to pass out any second.

"How'd you escape the bus?"

"Don't interview her," Kylie snaps.

Chase shoots her a cross look.

"She's in shock, moron." Kylie turns to me. "We've gotta get Liza to a—"

Liza's arm shoots up, clutches Kylie's wrist. "I didn't . . . escape." She coughs several times, then says, "They . . . they let me go." She touches the broken arrow. "But one of them got me on the way out." She grimaces. "I think God's gonna take me now. I feel it. I feel the cold."

Bear snaps out of his trance. Rubs his eyes, then jumps up. He walks over to Liza, hoists her up as if she were made of feathers. "You're not going anywhere yet." He wraps his arm around her backside, steadies her onto her feet. "Not until we get you to a hospital."

"Agreed," I say as I slide my arm around her as well. "Come on. Let's go."

Liza lets out another groan, talks incoherently. Something about Damien. Something about him being "all wrong." Hard to understand what she's rambling about because she keeps going in and out of consciousness.

"Guys, let's be real." Chase moves in front of the group. "She's going to slow us down!"

I say nothing for a beat. Glaring at this selfish little prick, part in surprise at his lack of care for others. Part in anger.

He'd make a good Chad.

My ex would probably go for a guy like this.

"Move," I tell him.

"Wait-wait-wait." Chase waves his arms in protest. "I thought we were running. What the crap happened to that plan?"

"The plan changed, asshole." Kylie steps forward and shoves Chase aside. "Now, do like the man said and move!"

We keep walking in the general direction that I assume we were already headed. Trying to use the moon as my guide, though the tall trees surrounding us make it a little difficult. It doesn't take long before Liza starts to get heavy, even with the two of us carrying her. Bear is doing most of the lifting, thank God, but he's huffing and breathing hard.

Chase runs in front of us again, turns and walks backward as he asks, "So where are we going, geniuses?" He spins in a circle, arms spread wide. "Don't know if you all noticed, but we kind of got turned around. Exactly which way is east, west, or wherever the hell we're headed?"

The sound of a bird chirping cuts through the woods. It's an unusual chirp. I can't quite describe it—

Another weird chirp.

All of us stop in our tracks.

"What's that?" Bear asks, looking up at the treetops.

Another chirp.

Not that I'm an ornithologist, but that definitely doesn't sound like any sort of bird I've ever heard before in my thirty-something years on this planet.

And typically when I hear birds chirping, it's accompanied by a sense of peace in my soul.

Not dread.

A distant chirp answers.

"That's the second weirdest sound I've heard all night," Chase says, and I completely agree with him.

Then it hits me. "They're signaling to one another."

"What?" Chase asks.

"We're being watched," I say. "Those hunters back there aren't the only ones playing this sick game."

"Damien . . ." Liza mumbles.

"Why does she keep saying that prick's name?" Chase asks.

Another flare rockets up into the sky. This time it's a little closer . .
.

And in the direction we were already headed.

"See," Kylie says. "We are going the right way."

We continue walking what we now know for sure is east.

"Yeah. Right," Chase says. "Headed right into their trap. You guys ever think about that?"

"We covered this already," Bear says, his words a little tauter. "This whole thing was a trap."

"Damiiiieeeeen . . ." Liza mutters, eyes slowly opening.

"Damien, what? Jesus! You're creeping me out, lady," Chase says. "Spit it out already!"

"Chase, if they don't kill you, I just might," Bear says with a definite growl in his tone. "I'm about done with—"

"Damien is coming for you all!" Liza suddenly blurts out.

We stop dead in our tracks.

"Please stop . . . I need . . ." Liza wheezes, her breathing ragged. "I need . . . I need a moment."

Chase and Kylie turn to face Liza.

"What did you say?" Chase asks.

"Damien." Tears stream down Liza's face as she strains to get the words out. "He's the one . . . who let me go."

"What? But how?" Kylie asks. "We heard him screaming."

62

"Yeah . . ." Liza says with a nod. "That's because they . . ." She gulps hard, her face slick with tears and sweat. Glistening under the red glow of these sinister woods. "That's because they scalped him."

"And he didn't die from that?" I ask.

Liza shakes her head no. "He begged to become one of them, so they scalped him. It was horrible." For a second, her mouth opens and closes, and no words come out. "I-I-I can't get that image . . . out of my head. Then they were going after me next . . . but Damien stood up . . . blood all over his face. He had no skin left on his head . . . only . . . only a feather!" She takes a deep breath. "And he was smiling. Asked them to let me go." She shudders in our arms. Eyes fluttering as if she's about to tap out.

"Liza!" Bear shouts. "Liza!"

Liza comes to, and says, "He said he's coming." She turns her head in my direction. "Said he's coming for you!"

In the moonlight, with the bone-white rays of light spilling down between the treetops, I can clearly see the cold seriousness in her eyes. Dread washes over me. I shiver at the thought of that crazed teenager, bathed in his own blood, helping these maniacs pick us off one by one.

Shaking off those feelings as best as possible, I muster as much confidence as I can generate with, "That's . . . that's not going to happen." I'm telling her this as well as myself.

Before Liza can utter another word, an arrowhead bursts through her neck. Blood sprays Bear and I as Liza's head flops back.

"Jeeeeeee-sus!" Chase backs away, turns and vomits.

Kylie covers her face with her hands.

Before Bear and I can react, a voice shouts from the pitch-black depths of the forest, "Jesus?"

It's a very familiar voice.

"Not quite, assholes!"

It's Damien.

11

Fight or Flight

Another arrowhead emerges from Liza's chest. Blood bubbles up from her lips. She lets out a gurgled cry, collapses.

"Get down!" I shout. We barely make it to the ground before a wave of arrows tears through the air and passes over us.

There's a moment of silence. The four of us lay frozen, bodies flat against the earth, breathlessly awaiting the next dreadful thing to happen. There's a soft thud near us. The sound of a rock or stone being tossed our way. My first thought is that someone or something landed next to us, but no further sounds are made. The unnerving stillness of the night continues for a few more minutes.

Distinct, high-pitched laughter pierces the quiet.

"Who in Christ's name is that?" Chase asks, his chin still slick with a sliver of vomit. He wipes it away.

"Damien," I say.

"Bullshit!" Chase says. "That kid's corpse is a pile of charcoal by now."

Kylie's gaze shifts between Chase and me.

The laughter draws closer.

"I bet when you pussies woke up this morning," Damien says, "you didn't think you'd end up in the boonies, hunted like rats."

"Yep," I say. "That's Damien all right."

"There's no way," Chase says. "That kid is as dead as we're about to be if we don't get the fuck out of here."

"Liza said he's alive," Kylie says.

"She was delusional!"

"Why would she say that, then?" Kylie asks.

"Because she was hurt." Chase suppresses a frustrated breath. "Pain will do that to you, you know?"

"Chase, Bear, Rainbow Brite . . . Rodney." Damien snorts and spits. "You're all about to get yourselves a nice haircut tonight."

"That sound like Damien to you?" I ask.

Chase stammers. Pauses. His brain suddenly not working. Then he mutters, "No-no-no-no-no-no-no. This can't be happening." He shuts his eyes tight. "I'm just dreaming. Sound asleep on the bus—"

Kylie grabs Chase by the shirt and yanks him close. Her words are very terse. "This is no dream. This is our shared nightmare. Now nut up, shut up, and chill the heck out. You're not helping." She releases him, and he just glares at her. Mouth agape. Eyes glossy with fear.

War cries call and answer from every corner of the woods like some sort of primitive alarm system.

"What's that?" Bear asks, looking around.

"Just a guess, but it seems Damien's signaled the others," I say. "They're surrounding us."

"And why'd they let him live?" Chase is no longer whispering.

"Talk a little louder," Bear says, "so you can ask them for yourself."

"So, what are our options?" Kylie asks me.

"Well, if we run now, we'll risk them loading our backs full of arrows." I lift my head up from behind the log, survey the area. It's just the ominous forest and that red fog floating along the ground. "I don't see any sign of them, but there's no telling how many of them are out there . . . waiting."

"And the other option?" Kylie asks.

"We let them come to us, and we fight."

"Oh no!" Chase wipes the sheen of sweat off his face. Dries his hand with his hair. "No fucking way we're going to fight them."

"We've got weapons," I remind him.

"Weapons? Yeah, you mean two hammers against God knows how many of those freaks!" Chase shakes his head. "Screw fighting. I say we run."

"If you think you can outrun an arrow"—Bear sweeps his hand toward the shroud of trees surrounding us—"happy trails. I'm sticking with Rodney."

"CHEK-TAH!"

Liza is suddenly standing over us. Mouth open so wide she could swallow a softball. Teeth glowing. Ravenous eyes flashing red and orange like unearthly strobe lights. The arrowhead still protruding from her neck, fresh blood trailing down its tip. She cocks her head to the side. Raises a tomahawk above her head, and my first thought is, Where did she get that from?

Oh yeah.

That soft thud.

One of the hunters tossed her a toma—

"Mooooooove!" Bear shoves me aside just as Liza brings the weapon down with such surprising force, the ground trembles.

"Liza!" Chase shouts. "What are you doing?" He asks this as if there's a remote possibility that she is going to issue a natural response given that she was dead moments ago and is now somehow still mobile with several arrows in her body, including one which no doubt hinders her ability to breathe.

"Chek-taaaaaah!" Liza hisses. "Chek-taaaaaaah—"

I jump up and swing my tomahawk. Stone meets bone. There's a loud crack. Liza spirals backward. The second her backside hits the dirt, I straddle her. She glares up at me, eyes smoldering like hot coals. Spittle and blood foaming at the corners of her mouth backlit by her neon teeth.

"I'm sorry." I bring down the tomahawk and with one deliberate blow . . . Liza hisses no more.

One of the hunters hiding within the trees lets out a war cry. Sounds as though he's right next to us. Several shadows emerge from all directions. All of them heading our way.

"Oh . . . shit," I mutter.

"Way to kill your own," Damien shouts from some corner of the woods.

"Oh my God!" Chase scrambles to his feet. "They're coming right at us!"

As their heavy footfalls draw in, we identify three hunters – two with spears, one with a tomahawk.

No bows and arrows . . . thankfully.

Everyone gets to their feet. Bear pushes Kylie and Chase aside. He points and says, "Get behind those palm trees."

Off to our left, a tight thicket of foxtail palms is the closest thing we have for cover.

"Whaaaaat?" Chase protests.

"You heard what he said! Move your ass!" I shout. "You're both unarmed."

Kylie leans down, takes Liza's tomahawk. "Not anymore."

"Screw this," Chase says, breaking past Kylie and Bear. "I'm not waiting around for us to get slaughtered!"

He takes off running.

"Chase!" I yell. "Chase! Dammit, come back! Chase!"

Too late.

He's already hauling ass, headed east . . .

Toward what? God only knows.

12

Dark Corners of the Mind

The hunters are almost upon us. Bear, Kylie, and I stand ready to fight or die. Three versus three, not including Damien, wherever the heck he is. My heart is pumping so hard I almost feel faint. Or maybe I'm just woozy from fear. Here I was . . . ready to take my own life because I let situations dictate my emotions. And now all I want to do is live.

What a coward.

If Kylie and Bear knew how scared I am, they might not be following me. They might be booking it alongside Chase. Sure, I've managed people within the safety of an office setting, but not under the duress of being slain by maniacs. I've conquered deadlines, but not the dead themselves.

Then again, I've succeeded in getting us this far.

Is this self-preservation? Have I regained my will to live?

Or am I merely driven to not let these strangers die at the hands of these men?

Doesn't matter right now. All I want to do is kick ass, find out who's behind this sick game, and shove this tomahawk down their throat.

In the thick of the shadows, three pairs of smoldering red eyes come to life, zigzagging in the air like fireflies as they make their way toward us. Teeth glowing as if they've swallowed glow-sticks. They shriek as they raise their weapons. A raspy "Chek-taaaaaaah," escapes their rotten mouths.

"They're coming!" Bear shouts.

We raise our weapons.

The hunters will be on us in three . . .

Two . . .

One.

Everything goes haywire. A blur of motion. A collision of shadows outlined in red by the mist. Bodies colliding like trucks hitting one another head-on with deadly force. One of the hunters slams into me, and we're earthbound. Our weapons go skidding off, disappearing into the brush. We roll around in the dirt. Both of us grunting, frantically struggling to get control. To get the upper hand. He grabs me, I grab him. He stinks. Smells of a sour mix of rotten meat and manure. He bares his fangs like a starved creature ready to chomp down on supper, but a quick left hook knocks that toothy smirk off his face. He yanks on my shoulders, and we roll over several times. Roll around for what feels like forever, but that's how fights feel—

Like an eternity. My martial-arts training taught me that. But it didn't teach me how to deal with maniacal natives from purgatory.

Or wherever they're from.

His bony elbow clips my chin. I wince. The pain is instant and bright, traveling from my jawline into my brain. Suddenly he's on top of me. He brings up both hands, curls them into fists, and is about to hammer me into next week when I jab two fingers into his windpipe. Not sure if these guys breathe or not.

No matter.

The strike worked.

He gasps, cups his throat with both hands and it's all the time I need to prop up both feet against my butt and buck him off me. He quickly recovers, but so do I, and now we're squaring off.

Behind us, I hear Bear and Kylie taking on the other hunters. I want to jump in, help them out, but can't break away. Stinky here whips out a knife of sorts. It doesn't appear to be made of metal, but all I can make out is that it's sharp and I don't want it ending up inside of me. He makes several swipes, but I step backward with each swing. I'm praying that there's nothing behind me to either back into, or cause me to trip. Either one would suck.

He issues several more jabs. I dodge them all. Yeah, I'm still alive, but evading his attacks is wearing me out. My heart slams against my chest. Throat dry as Death Valley. Ears throbbing.

The hunter winds up, haymaker style. He takes one big swing at my throat . . . and muscle memory takes over. I step inside the arc of his motion. With all his energy dumped into that single attack, his body leans forward just enough for me to catch his arm, bring it to my chest, and flip him over—still holding on to him the entire time. He crashes hard into the dirt, face-first, his arm breaking as he lands.

He lets out a deathly wail.

I spin around, using his shoulder as a pivot point, and break his arm a second time. The grip on his knife loosens. I steal it from him and plunge it into the back of his head. The soft spot. Right where the skull and the base of the neck meet.

He dies instantly.

I pull the knife back out. Dark blood glistens on the shaft. Indeed, the blade is not metal, but bone. Animal bone? Human bone? No idea. All I know is that it is sharp and it did the trick.

"Rodney!" Kylie cries out behind me.

I spin around and find her on the ground. Her hands holding the pointy end of a spear inches away from her stomach. A hunter stands above her, legs straddling either side of her hips. He's pushing down with all his body weight, trying to drive the spear into her.

I charge at him, surprising myself with my own speed, and drive the bone blade up through the base of his skull just as I did with Mr. Stinky over there. This guy jiggles in place, releases the spear. When he stops moving, I retrieve my blade and push his corpse to the side.

Both Kylie and I take a moment to catch our breath. To digest what just happened. Can't believe I just took down those hunters the way I did. Guess what my old buddy Phil said was true: we fall to the level of our training. Those years hitting the mat were worth more than just stress relief.

I extend a hand and pull Kylie to her feet. There's blood on her face. Oh God. "You're bleeding," I say as I reach toward her face.

"I'm fine!" she huffs and knocks my hand aside.

We both hear Bear grunt, and turn to see him lift a hunter up in the air like some WWE wrestler. Bear tosses him onto a large tree stump. The hunter cries out as his spine is crunched against the solid wood. Before the hunter can make another sound, Bear crushes in his face with one swift blow of his tomahawk.

But the beating goes on for longer than it needs to.

"Bear!" I yell.

Bear continues hammering down into the hunter's head until it's oatmeal.

"Jesus! Bear . . . enough!" I pull him away from the hunter's mutilated body. "He's dead, all right?"

Bear's massive shoulders heave with each breath, he trades glances between the hunter and me. He gives the corpse a final look then tosses the tomahawk onto the ground.

"I killed him just like this," Bear says, his voice shaky.

"What?" I ask.

"I smashed his head in."

"Yeah, I know! We just saw—"

"No. Not him," Bear says. "Jake."

I share a look with Kylie, and then back to Bear whose gaze drifts downward.

"Who's Jake?" I ask.

"The asshole who talked me into knocking over a convenience store." Bear gazes straight ahead now. The shock of this situation unlocking some dark corner of his mind. "I didn't expect there'd be a pregnant girl behind the register." He's focusing with such intent that I'm compelled to check out what he's staring at, but there's nothing out there but more of that red glow. He finally turns back to us. "I thought he was just going to tie her up while I went and got the money."

I hear movement in the shadows.

This is a terrible time for Bear to have a breakdown.

"Bear..." I try to cut him off, but he continues.

"Jake had the goddamn nerves of a squirrel." Bear takes in a deep breath. "The girl moved like she was going for something, and he shot her."

I hear that distinct, shrill bird call of a war cry. Damien. He's calling out for his buddies. For reinforcements. But no one is responding.

Damien is alone.

"Bear, I believe you," I say. "Now snap out of it, man."

Damien cries out. His strident war call is unnerving. The hairs on my arms stand on end.

"Bear!" I shake him. He may as well be rooted into the ground. The man barely moves. "Look, we need to go!"

"Yeah, come on!" Kylie pleads.

"I deserve to die for my sins," Bear mutters, seemingly not hearing a single word we're saying. "That noose should've held around my neck."

Damien lets out another war cry.

This time at least a dozen hunters answer. Well . . . a dozen is just a guess, but it sure sounds like more than one or two.

"Bear," I say, "we are leaving!"

But Bear snatches up my collar, bunching it in his hands. For a moment, I fear he's going to punch me, but instead he just says, "My name's Arthur. Bear's my last name." As he speaks, I get the feeling in my gut that we've lost him mentally. "If I die, tell Sasha and my little girls that I'm sorry I couldn't make it home."

"You're not going to die, all right? You're going to live to see your family!"

He gawks at me as if I'm speaking another language. As if the idea of peace is so remote, that the whole concept seems unattainable now.

"By this time tomorrow, you'll be curled up with Sasha on the sofa, watching The Late Show." I catch a glimmer of sanity in Bear's eyes. Seems he's listening to me now. "You'll be kissing the top of your children's heads as they rest quietly in their beds."

Under the sliver of light from the moon and the red haze, I watch as Bear's distant expression fades. A weak smile spreads across his lips. A moment of serenity and sanity?

Maybe he believes me?

I'm about to tell him to get a move on when that peaceful look on his face is replaced by fear. "Look out!" Bear pushes me aside, launching me sideways into the dirt.

This is quickly followed by a wet thud—the sound of something solid hitting something else very solid.

Followed by Bear crying out in pain.

13

Not So Fast, Lover Boy

I look up to see Bear howling above me. The long end of a spear protruding from his stomach. He grabs it with both hands, screaming in agony.

"Bear!" Kylie yells. "Nooooooo!"

Bear's face contorts. The beads of sweat on his skin shimmer under the moonlight, outlining the pained grimace. He pulls the end of the spear from out his belly and holds the weapon in the air, just as the hunters have.

"Come . . . Come at me!" Bear roars. "Come at me, motherfuckers!"

War cries answer from all around the forest. A stampede of feet trampling over the twigs and leaves soon follows.

Bear looks down at us, eyeballs swelling to the size of moons. His words are very distinct and deliberate. "What are you waiting for?"

I can barely speak. My gaze shifts down to the glistening, growing bloodstain on his shirt. Then I look back at him.

"I said, what are you waiting for?" he asks again. "RUN!"

"We're not leaving you!"

Bear pulls Kylie and me to our feet. I swear the man has the strength of a god. Only gods don't bleed, and he's doomed if we don't get him to a hospital—

"I said . . . RUUUUUUUUUUN!"

The stampede of hunters draws closer.

I put a hand on Bear's shoulder, not wanting to abandon this man, but he swats my hand away. Tears welling in his eyes. "GODDAMMIT!" He gives me a shove that nearly knocks me off my feet. "GET OUT OF HERE, RODNEY!"

The war cries are nearly on top of us.

Without further prodding, Kylie and I take off running at a speed that would make horses jealous. Cutting through trees and tall bushes with the precision, agility, and determination of smart missiles locked on to their respective bull's eyes—only Kylie and I have no idea where are our target destination is.

Nor what lies beyond the wall of trees ahead.

"THAT'S RIGHT, ASSHOLES!" Bear cries out behind us. "COME GET SOME!"

This is followed by a frightening chorus of war cries, then sounds of Bear belting out himself, then a series of hoots and howls.

Then the deathly silence, broken up only by our feet thumping against the ground and the huffs of our own heaving breaths. We run for what feels like another few miles, and then I hit my wall. Exhaustion kicks in. I stop running, and Kylie spins around. I bend over, prop both hands on my knees and catch my breath . . . or at least try to.

"I'm sorry," I say between gasps, "my side is cramping up bad."

"Mine too, but we've got to keep going," she says, equally winded.

"Keep going?" I say, still panting. "Kylie, I don't even know where we are going."

She swallows a few big breaths of air, then points up ahead. "Take a look."

And I see where she's pointing, off in the east. I don't know how I didn't see them before—perhaps due to fear or adrenaline—but there's a break in the forest, and up ahead are . . .

Lights.

"There's something over there," she says as she puts her hand on my back. "Now come on!"

I nod. She's right. For as tired as I am, to take a break now—even a quick one—would be suicide.

Suicide.

Hmm...

Here I was, ready to end my life.

Now I find that I want to live.

Never has air tasted better than after running for my life. Maybe that's the whole point of this game. To teach us something about gratitude.

That or for someone to get their jollies off on killing strangers.

I'd love to take the more philosophical route, but no doubt the latter reasoning is clearly the motivation for this manhunt. But why?

What's the point?

"RODNEY!" a voice cries out from behind us.

Damien's voice.

"STOP RUNNING, YOU PUSSY!"

He's not that far away.

"That's our cue," Kylie says, taking my hand. "Come on!"

That blink of a breather was enough to barely let me get my wind back, but that break may have given Damien just enough time to close in on us. Doesn't matter. We take off, not wanting to stick around to find out.

After another ten minutes of running, my lungs and legs burn. Both of us stumble through the woods like drunks after a hard night of partying. I'm still grateful for the full moon and the funky red glow all around us. We'd literally be running in the dark otherwise.

Just as we are about to collapse, we see a break in the trees. Further ahead, a large field, and in the center is a small RV park. Several light poles encircle the outer edges of the park. It's odd seeing an RV park in the middle of nowhere like this, with no major roads leading to it, but here it sits. About a dozen trailers quietly nestled close to one another.

Only one of them has lights on inside.

"Think this is where the flares came from?" Kylie asks.

"It would make sense," I say. "Then again, nothing tonight has made sense."

Kylie turns to me, and the ambient light from the RV park cascades across her face. The sweat on her forehead sparkles like glitter. She's still catching her breath, mouth slightly open. There's a certain depth in those eyes—a depth I don't think I've seen in a woman before.

Certainly not in Diane.

And maybe that was a red flag that I should've paid attention to from the beginning. Diane was shallow. Diane lied to me. And her superficiality led to the end of our marriage. She told me she had walls up and that I needed to be patient. That she had gone through some shit when she was a kid, but that was far from the truth.

The truth was that Diane had walled herself away from anyone that could get to her heart.

Namely me.

Kept me an outsider for all those years, only to cheat on me and throw me away like a stranger.

But I see the opposite in Kylie's eyes.

There's warmth there. Substance. All things Diane was devoid of.

I don't know how I know this about Kylie, but I know. See it plain as a billboard off a highway. Maybe it's because we saw the face of death tonight and that's enough to make all the phony, insignificant stuff disappear. Our horrifying reality is boiling out the impurities—the trivial crap rising to the top to be scraped off. I guess it's accurate to say that having my life flash before my eyes peel back a layer of the world I didn't realize I wasn't seeing. Or perhaps I'd just been too wrapped up in trying to scale the impossibly high walls of someone who didn't want to be loved.

Diane's walls were never mine to try to climb over.

The bullet I was going to take for her infidelity, my loss of her affection—what little there was—would've been taken in vain.

Being brought to the brink of death is shedding light on what really matters.

Family.

Friends.

Love.

Love?

I feel excitement stir in the back of my mind. Correction: the center of my mind. The temporal lobes of my brain are already picturing a future with Kylie. This stranger that I've just met. Maybe it's managerial sixth sense that I innately possess—the same instinctual insight that was 100 percent accurate during interviews. Generally, within the first few minutes of meeting a candidate for a position, I knew right away if they'd be the right fit for the job or not. Dating is similar to interviewing in that respect.

And I've only been wrong once.

Thanks, Diane.

There's something about Kylie that draws me. A spark somewhere in my cerebral cortex that tells me . . .

Wait a minute.

What am I doing?

Warmth spreads across my face. I suddenly feel like I'm staring at Kylie too hard.

"Rodney?" she asks. "You all right there?"

I shake my head; shake off the thoughts. "Uh, yeah," I say as I wipe the sweat from my brow. Way to play it smooth, Casanova. "Just taking a moment."

"I'll admit it," Kylie says. "I'm freaking out inside." She is? Well, she has a heck of a way of keeping her fear suppressed. Which is the polar opposite of Chase.

I feel this undeniable urge to console her, to cup her face in my hands and kiss her forehead, and tell her that everything's going to be all right. That we're going to make it out of this alive. That I might be bold enough to ask her out for coffee. Then at some point, I might be lucky enough to take her out to dinner. But for starters, that would be awkward, and she'd probably punch me into next week.

And secondly, the last two people I said would live through this ended up dying.

"I thought I wanted to die," she says as she looks away. "And now all I want to do is live." She turns back to me. Her gaze searching my face for answers.

"Well then let's keep moving." I nod toward the RV park ahead. "So that we can make sure that happens."

Just as I'm about to pull her beyond the edge of the woods and into the clearing, a hand grabs my shoulder, and I hear Damien's pitchy voice scream, "NOT SO FAST, LOVER BOY!"

14

Tomahawks & Fireworks

Damien spins me around to face him, and I get a full view of his newfound condition. The top of his skull is exposed. Strings of muscle and skin still attached. A dark web of flesh, what I can only guess was once part of his scalp, hangs from the back of his head like a backward ball cap. Stripes of blood run down his face. His skin, pale and waxy. He's equal parts nauseating and disturbing.

"Go!" I shout to Kylie as Damien pulls me so close enough I can smell his blood.

His eyes light up. A full spectrum of orange and reds. He raises a tomahawk above his head.

"Kylie—GO!" Out of the corner of my eye, I catch Kylie do a double take as if unsure she heard me right.

She takes off running for the RV park.

Damien's eyes dart in her direction—

I plunge the bone knife into his stomach.

He freaks. Plants a foot in my chest and kicks me backward. I land on my tailbone. The sharp pain is intense. For a second, I wonder if he cracked my back, but thankfully I'm still able to move.

"You really think this little splinter is gonna kill me?" Damien yanks the knife out of his gut and tosses it aside. He stands above me now with those demonic eyes, glaring down at me through fresh streaks of drying blood. "You can't kill me, dumbass!"

"What are you talking about?"

"I'm immortal now." His teeth pulse a dull white as he finishes with, "Chek-tah!"

I wish I knew what that meant.

Or maybe I don't want to know what Chek-tah means.

"I'm immortal," he repeats, "and you're not!" With that, he raises the tomahawk above his head once again.

Damien might be immortal or whatever, but apparently he still feels pain. Before he can strike, I bring my leg up and kick him square in the kneecap. Damien buckles slightly and howls out in agony.

I roll to my side and get to my feet, and I throw a clumsy, backward kick knocking him to the ground. I take off running. Just as I break through the wall of trees and into the clearing, I feel bony fingers grab my shoulder. He catches me by my shirt—the tips of his fingers light up like matches. Fingernails sizzling, skin cracking, and turning a fiery amber. Damien screams. Pulls his hand to his chest, recoiling as if he'd touched a hot stove. There's a bewildered expression on his grotesque face. Beyond the pain, he's trying to figure out what just happened.

And so am I . . .

For a moment.

I make a mad dash for the RV park.

"Rodney!" Damien shouts.

I glance back to see a twirling tomahawk headed right at me. I feel every nerve on my body twinge. Bracing for impact. I shut my eyes. This is it—

Pop!

It's like the sound of a clay pigeon bursting in midair.

I spin on my heels to see a cloud of cascading ashes spill onto the ground.

Damien just stands there. Speechless. Guess his tomahawk wasn't supposed to burst like a firecracker.

He belts out a war cry, chants in a throaty language I've never heard.

Begins moving rhythmically, as if dancing to a song stuck in his head. There's a lot of foot stomping, face twisting, and tongue wagging. Very reminiscent of the haka performed by the Maori rugby team of New Zealand before a match.

A dance of intimidation.

It's almost . . . mesmerizing watching him do his thing.

Part of me screams to keep running. The other part of me is frozen with unexplainable curiosity. I guess that part of me is dying to uncover what this whole game is about.

A dozen hunters, armed with spears, emerge from the woods and line up next to Damien. They dance alongside him, eyes pulsing brightly with their shades of rage. Tongues wagging. Fists thumping against chests. They chant the occasional, "Aaaah-ooooohhh!"

The hairs on my entire body stand on end as I watch them move.

Run, Rodney.

They stop abruptly, raise their spears, and take aim in my direction.

OK . . . so I should've run.

I turn back toward the RV park and haul ass.

Damien lets out this weird yodel, and the other hunters all respond in unison with a resounding, "CHEK-TAAAAAAAAAAAHHHHHH!"

My skin tingles as I expect at any second I'll have several spears bursting through my chest. I'm running as fast as I can. My legs and lungs are on fire. Ears are throbbing so hard I can hear my own pulse.

The RV park is almost within reach.

I hear several small explosions behind me. I glance back, expecting a rainstorm of spears, but instead see a dozen clouds of ash, again dissipating like spent bottle rockets. I stop dead in my tracks, bewildered at why their weapons disintegrated in midair.

Damien and the hunters watch me with the snarling gaze of junkyard mutts trapped behind an invisible fence line. Some bare their glowing fangs, some mumble, some chant, and some remain motionless. I expect at any moment they'll charge across the field and fight me hand-to-hand.

But instead, they do the opposite and fade back into the forest. Some glancing over their shoulders as they do.

Damien is the last to disappear.

"Run all you want, pussy!" he shouts. "But you'll be dead before dawn!"

Yeah. Says the little bitch who ran away himself.

I continue toward the RV park.

"You hear me, Rodney?" Damien screams at the top of his lungs. "YOU'RE FUCKING DEAD!"

When I make it, I look back at the woods. They're all gone now. Including Damien. For whatever reason, they didn't follow me. And their weapons disappeared mid-air . . .

Why?

There's more to this game than Jim Grimm let on.

I head into the park, careful to stay close to the exterior walls of the first trailer I come up to. Don't want to risk getting spotted. My luck with the locals so far hasn't exactly been stellar, and I don't want to take any chances.

Most of the trailers still have their lights off. Then again, that makes sense considering what time it most likely is—although the noise of the hunters would have woken most people. What I find most odd is that there's only one automobile parked nearby—a beat-up old Ford. Either the owner's the only one with a vehicle in the park, or the only one living in the park.

Most of the trailers are in rough shape. Mother Nature has had her way with them, and she wasn't gentle about it. Some are surrounded by thick walls of grass. Some have vines snaking up their sidewalls, making the trailers appear more like ruins than inhabitable spaces. Several tall light posts shine down a yellowish-brown light, casting a murky brume over everything.

I wonder where Kylie disappeared to? Did she make it? Did something get to her? I'm not a very religious man, but right now, I'm praying to God she's ok.

I slip around the corner and come to what appears to be the center of the park. There I come to the only trailer with its lights on—the same trailer Kylie, and I first saw when we got to the clearing. I press myself against its damp, aluminum walls. The dank aroma of old cigarette smoke, polyester, and mold is everywhere. I nearly gag. I move around to the back wall of the trailer, where I catch some activity near a large window—shadows pacing back and forth inside. Then voices. One male and one female. I creep up to the window and peek inside.

Kylie and Chase are very much alive! She stands with her arms crossed as Chase storms back and forth, gesturing erratically.

I'm about to tap on the window and call out their names when I feel something cold kiss the back of my neck.

"Unless you can outrun a double-barrel shotgun at close range," says the creaky voice of an old man behind me, "I suggest you do exactly as I say."

15

Ancient Story-time

"Now put your arms up," the old man says, "and move." He jabs the barrel into the base of my skull, and I see stars. "I said move!"

"All right!" I do as told.

The old man walks me around to the front of the trailer. "Open it," he says with a painful prod of the gun into the center of my spine. "It's unlocked."

I open the door, and I'm hit with that overwhelming stale odor of cigarettes and mold. The stench so strong, I wince. When Chase and Kylie see me, they stop mid-conversation.

"Rodney?" Kylie says, her face lighting up with relief.

She moves like she's about to hug me or something when the old man barks, "No! The two of you—sit!"

Chase and Kylie retreat to a coffee-brown sofa, armrests black and dingy, just like the rest of the place. Near their feet is a worn coffee table adorned with a massive circular ashtray holding a mountain of twisted cigarette butts.

The old man sticks the barrel into the center of my back. I grimace as a spike of pain lights up my spine. "Go sit with them on the couch!"

I shoot him a dirty look as I squeeze in between Chase and Kylie.

The old man plops himself down on a rocking chair. It groans under his weight. His long, gray hair is matted, greasy, and clings to his scalp in thin bunches. His skin is weathered, pockmarked. He looks like an old-school rocker well past his touring days. He lights up a cigarette, hand shaking as he holds it to his crusty lips.

"Getting old"—he takes a puff—"sucks. Everything hurts. Everything creaks."

I survey the room. Old faded pictures decorate the walls. Black and white photos of, no doubt, people who've come and gone in this old man's life. He rests the shotgun on his lap, barrel still pointed in our direction. He blows out a cloud of smoke, coughs several times, and clears his throat.

"You might not feel so old if you'd taken better care of yourself," Chase says, nodding toward the old man's cigarette.

The old man swats the air in Chase's direction. "Shut up, pretty boy. You're lucky you made it this far yourself." He props a crooked thumb against his chest and says, "I smelled the dried piss in your pants a mile away. If I smelled it, you know they smelled it, too."

Chase turns red. Eyes his crotch, then exchanges looks with us, embarrassed.

"So what's your name?" the old man asks me.

"Rodney."

"Rodney . . . eh?" He leans forward in his seat, offers his hand. The cigarette bobs up and down in his mouth as he speaks. "Name's Mac. Mac Wiley." I hesitate, and he seemingly picks up on what I'm thinking. "It's OK, son. I'm not going to shoot you . . . not yet," he says with another chuckle.

We shake. His hand is cold and clammy. A wet, dead fish.

"And who exactly are you?" I ask. "Mac?"

"The maintenance man. I take care of odds and ends. Whatever needs to be done." Mac leans back in his seat, takes another drag. "I was telling these two earlier that y'all have made it farther than anyone else has in years."

"How did you know that I was outside your trailer?"

"Because they told me." Mac nods toward the window. "Your hunting party. Last time I heard that much commotion from the

Kenneh'wah, a man about your age fell at my feet right outside my front door." He shakes his head as he recalls that event. "Poor fellow had about three arrow holes in his back."

"Wait . . . Kenneh-what?" I ask.

"Kenneh'wah. Not Kenneh-what."

"Whatever. Who are they?"

Mac freezes in his chair as if he heard a noise outside.

"What is it?" Chase asks, his words rushed. "Is it them?"

Mac relaxes, takes another drag of his cigarette. With a light chuckle, he replies, "If you mean them as in rats—yes. Those bastards are everywhere. Climbing inside my walls. Making tunnels in my insulation." He suddenly rises and raps the end of the shotgun against his ceiling as if it were a broom. "Move somewhere else!" He shouts up at the roof as he knocks against it several more times. "There's a whole goddamn forest out there for you! So, get out of my home, you hear me?"

Kylie, Chase and I look at one another. The expressions on their faces tell me that they're thinking what I'm thinking.

I jump out of my seat, yank the shotgun from Mac's hands, and point it at his face. "Now's your turn to sit down, Grandpa."

Mac freezes once again. A crooked smile forms on his face. He appears more amused than afraid. There's a tinge of insult in his voice as he mutters, "Grandpa? Grandpa? Now that would imply that I got children, which I don't." He calmly sits down, snuffs out his cigarette, and leans back in his rocker. Folding his hands over his lap as if he's about to tell us a bedtime story. "Well?" He gestures for me to continue. "Go ahead. Ask away. I know you have questions."

"Who are these men hunting us?"

"I told you—the Kenneh'wah." Mac smirks as he continues. "They're the tribe that once inhabited these grounds centuries ago. They still think this is their land."

"What do you mean once?"

"You don't have to point that gun at me." A taut grin stretches across Mac's face. "I'm more than happy to tell you what you want to know. I haven't had visitors since . . ." He trails off, scratches his chin. There's a noise up in the ceiling that catches his attention. "God . . . damn . . . rats!" He starts to get up, but I shove him back down into his chair. His upper lip twitches. A scowl forms. There's a wicked darkness in his eyes. Two bottomless pits, full of the vapid emptiness of a man who's seen and done more than he'll ever admit to.

I've seen that look before.

In the wild, distant eyes of serial killers on the news.

Blank gazes void of any remorse or emotional accountability for their actions.

I don't trust him. Not one bit. The stale smell and ragged condition of this trailer confirm that he has been here a while. Judging by his haggard appearance, I doubt he gets out much.

"Go on." I keep the gun on him.

Mac lets out an annoyed huff. "Back in the fifteen hundreds, this was Kenneh'wah territory. They were a small tribe. Kept to themselves. Relatively unknown. That was until a wandering band of Spaniards came along in search of gold in the area." He leans toward the table, reaching for something. I raise the shotgun, gesturing that I will split him like an atom. "Jumping Jesus on a pogo stick! I just wanna grab me another smoke. You mind?"

I pause, then sit back down. Gun still trained on him.

"You ought to get those nerves in check." Mac lights up.

"Not after what we've been through tonight."

"Those people got what they wanted," he says with a shrug. "They got to die."

Without a second thought, I launch at him and bring the butt of the shotgun down on his hand, pinning it to the table. Mac cries out, the yelp of an old hound. The limp cigarette spills out of his mouth and bounces on the floor. I snub it out quickly.

"JEEEE-SUS!" Mac shrieks. He goes on a tirade, telling me that I'm an asshole, that I broke his hand, blah, blah, blah. He bares his rotten teeth as he rants. They're decorated with a patina of black-and-blue decay. A row of century-old tombstones tightly packed together, battered by Mother Nature and crumbling from years of acid rain.

Or, in his case, a ferocious appetite for nicotine.

I lean close and gaze into Mac's soulless eyes. "Continue." I release him and sit back down, all while keeping the business end of the shotgun squarely aimed at him.

"Like I was saying!" Mac sneers as he holds his hand against his chest as if it's an injured dove. "The Spaniards came looking for gold. Instead, they found another treasure . . . a campground full of Native American women of all ages." His gaze trails down to the ashtray, eyes lighting up as though he were staring at a succulent rack of ribs and not a mound of cigarette butts. "Them girls had caramel skin. Voluptuous bodies, tight and ripe." He chuckles to himself as he looks up at me. "Ha, ha, ha. I mean the young ones, not the old ones."

My grip tightens around the shotgun.

An uneasy laugh escapes Mac, and he continues. "Yeah, so, unfortunately, these yoga-bodied beauties were laid ripe for the picking . . . and raping. Most of the males in their tribe had gone off hunting. Only a handful of men in the village kept watch—the very old and the very young. Didn't take much for the Spaniards to overwhelm them." He licks his lips as if reliving the event in his mind. There's a thirst in his tone that unnerves me. "Then it was on with the fiesta! Them Spaniards had a hall pass to have their way with those women." He stops talking abruptly and gapes at his injured hand. "I can't believe you actually broke it—"

I hop up, flip the coffee table over, ashes and cigarette butts flying everywhere. I level the shotgun with his eyeballs.

"KEEP TALKING!" I shout.

Mac glowers.

"I SAID, KEEP TALKING!"

"Piss off."

I kick his shin.

He cries out. "Gard-dammit!" Rubs his leg. "All right, all right! For Christ's sake—relax, asshole!" Mac holds both hands up in protest. "When the Kenneh'wah hunters came back, they found their village burned to the ground and their people slaughtered. Men, women, and children. They wanted revenge. But the Spaniards had been hiding. They ambushed the hunters. Cut them down with their guns. The Keeneh'wah never had a chance to get their vengeance."

"But why rape the women?" Kylie asks. "Why kill off the tribe entirely? They weren't hurting anybody."

Mac turns to her. "Sweetie." She makes a sour face at the word sweetie. "Because they could."

"Maybe they killed them out of frustration?" Chase asks. "Because they didn't find any gold?"

Mac smacks his knee as he laughs. "I'm sure that didn't help!"

"How's that funny?" I ask, holding back every iota of wanting to beat the crap out of this geriatric sack of shit.

"Because it is! Look, nobody cares. It's ancient history," Mac says with a casual shrug. "That all went down before your great-great-great-great-great grandfather was more than sperm in his father's nut sack—"

Kylie punches Mac. The old man squeals. Cups his face with his hand.

"You're the asshole!" she snaps.

Mac jumps to his feet as if to hit her, but I press the barrel of the shotgun against his crooked nose.

"Touch her," I say through gritted teeth, "and I'll paint the wall with your brains."

Mac's mouth twitches. Hands curl into fists. I'm sure he wants to try me, but as close as I am, I'd split open his head like a cantaloupe.

Outside several war cries echo from the forest.

Chase stiffens. He turns to the window. "Oh great." Then turns back to us and mutters, "They're coming."

Without taking his eyes off my gun barrel, Mac says, "No, they're not."

"Huh?" Chase looks at Mac. "They're not?"

"No, sir. They're waiting for you guys to make your next move." Mac scowls. "You mind getting that out of my face now?"

I hesitate, then step back, and lower the gun.

Mac slinks into his chair.

"Why are they waiting on us?" I ask. "Why not attack us now?"

"Because they can't!" Spittle flies out of Mac's mouth. "Wake up, son! Didn't you find it odd that they didn't chase after you?"

I nod.

"And that they didn't put an arrow or a damn spear in your backside?"

"Well actually," I say, "they tried."

"And what happened?"

"Their weapons crumbled in the air like they were made of . . . dust."

Mac says nothing. His gaze trailing off into another world.

"And why's that?" I ask.

Mac sticks his index finger up in the air, makes a small circle with it. "There's a protection spell over the RV park."

"A what?" Chase asks, his voice making that signature crack of his.

"Kind of part of the maintenance program here. I gotta cast the spell every morning for it to stay in effect."

"You're a magician?" Kylie asks, eyebrow raised.

"Ha! No. I'm the maintenance man. It's just some Kenneh'wah mumbo jumbo that the shaman told me to say." Mac looks toward the window. "Everything past those light poles surrounding the park is Kenneh'wah soil. Same dirt on which their blood was spilled." Under his breath, "Well, technically, this whole area is their land. The spell just keeps them temporarily at bay from entering the RV parks."

"Parks?" I ask.

Mac clears his throat. "I meant park."

This scumbag is a terrible liar. There's more than one park. Makes sense. I'm assuming that someone smarter, or at least less senile, is orchestrating this whole thing.

"So basically this is all one big burial ground?" Chase asks.

Mac laughs, his Adam's apple rising and falling beneath his leathery skin.

Chase searches our faces as if he has somehow missed the joke.

"A burial ground would imply that they were buried." Mac leans forward, sneers at Chase.

"O . . . K?"

"OK, so"—Mac's eyes twinkle with delight as he continues—"weren't you listening, son? The Kenneh'wah were murdered. The bodies that weren't consumed by the fire when the village burned down were left in the sun to rot. To be picked apart by the vultures, the rodents, the ants. The maggots and the worms."

Another war cry in the distance.

It's as if the Kenneh'wah know we're talking about them.

"Not a very honorable death for a warrior," Mac says flatly, seemingly numb to the escalating commotion in the background. "They went to their graves with wrath in their hearts, having never gotten their revenge." Mac taps his chin. "I think there's even something in the Bible about going to bed angry. Something about not letting the sun go down while you're still mad. Well, the Kenneh'wah did just that."

"Whoa," Chase says. "Hold on a second, Moses—"

"Mac!"

"Whatever!" Chase squints, pinches the bridge of his nose as if fighting back a headache. "You're saying that a tribe of Indians has risen from the dead to hunt down random people as payback for some sort of century-old PTSD?"

Mac throws his head back, laughs once again. My grip tightens around the shotgun. How dare this jerk-off make light of this whole situation? Laughing about those who'd lost their lives, both in the past . . .

And present.

"This is just one big joke to you, isn't it?" I level the shotgun at Mac's face, but he doesn't flinch.

"Relax, Romeo," Mac says. "I'm laughing because your buddy pretty much nailed it, all right?" He lowers his arms. "Well . . . I mean . . . except for a few things."

"Like...?""

"Like . . . well . . . they don't like to be called Indians. Kind of derogatory, ya know? They are Kenneh'wah—"

I gesture with the shotgun that I've had enough of his antics. He puts his arms up in protest. "Get to the point!"

"OK! OK!"

"We haven't got all night."

"You're right about that." Another little giggle escapes Mac, and I jam the butt of the shotgun down on his foot as though I were nailing it to the floor. He cries out, pulls his leg up close to his body. "SHEEEEEITTTT!" His face turns red, veins bulging along his temples, holding back the rush of pain as he blurts out, "For Pete's sake, I ain't getting any replacement bones in this lifetime, so stop breaking the ones I got!"

"You'll be all right," I say without an ounce of pity in my voice.

"What are you, a doctor? Doctor Rodney?"

"Finish what you were saying, Mac!" Kylie snaps. I shoot her a look of surprise, and she shrugs. Under her breath, "Old fart's got an ADHD problem."

Mac takes a deep breath, doing his best to suppress the pain as he goes on. "Look . . . them hunting ya . . . it ain't personal. The Kenneh'wah simply see you as chek-tah."

"Chek-tah. Yeah, we keep hearing that," Chase says. "What's that mean?"

Mac spits out the word. "Invader."

"Invader?"

"Yeah, pretty boy. You're invading their land, and you're not welcome."

"Really?" Chase jumps to his feet, points at himself. "For the record, I didn't ask to be here! None of us did."

"But you did." Mac's eyes darken. He stretches his leg out and lets out a grunt. "You all did." All pain seems to evaporate from the old man's face, replaced by something sinister. His nostrils flare, his eyelids narrow, and he bares his rotten teeth as he goes on. "The moment you all started thinking about killing yourselves, the shaman picked up on your intention like a bogey on a psychic radar."

Chase makes a face, pulling his chin inward and shaking his head as if he just tasted something foul. He mutters, "I never wanted to kill myself."

Mac eyes him with the stoic gaze of a judge who's heard this story one too many times.

Chase glances over at Kylie and me, searching our expressions. All I read from him is fear and shame. He turns back to Mac. "I love my life. I love what I do. I'm a happy man, and I'll be happier once I'm out of this fucking nightmare!"

"Whatever you want to tell yourself is fine by me." Mac leans back in his chair, shoulders relaxing. "The shaman picked up on your energy. Subconsciously guide you here. Hell . . . you might have even met the man and didn't even know it."

"Bullshit!" Chase shouts. "No voodoo magic curse brought us here. No witch doctors or suicidal intentions. None of that crap. You and your sicko friends did that." There's a quiver in his tone that betrays his words. As if he is unsure he believes in what he's saying himself.

"Well, yeah. They're the other half of the formula." Mac turns to me. "Mind if I have a smoke now?"

"How about I give you one of your throw pillows to huff on?" I ask. "There's enough nicotine in it to kill a cow."

"Oh sure," Mac mumbles under his breath. "Pick on an innocent old man."

"Innocent? Are you serious? You're a part of this game."

"You're not so innocent, yourself . . . Rodney." There's a snarky grin on his face as he asks, "Tell me . . . what does the barrel of Berretta taste like?"

I feel the blood drain from my face.

How the hell?

I glance back at Kylie. There's an expression of surprise in those beautiful eyes of hers. Before I can utter a word in defense, Mac chimes in again. "Your sister saved your ass, didn't she?"

I spin around to face him. "How did you know that?"

"The shaman picked up on your thoughts. As soon as you wanted to kill yourself—and meant it—he picked up on your intent, fed on it, and was able to subconsciously influence those related to you—including your sister—and bring you right to us."

"What?" This is too much to process. "No way. Becky wouldn't do that!" My gaze falls to the floor, mind sputtering like an engine low on gas. "I agree with Chase. This is . . . this is bullshit."

Mac waves his good hand in the air. "Yet here you all are . . . running for your lives."

Trying to sort through this is too much to handle in one night. Besides, we're not here to solve a mystery. We're here to find a way out.

Snapping out of my stupor, I ask, "Who is this shaman?"

"A reluctant participant who owes Baxter a lot of money, so this is his penance."

"Baxter?"

Mac makes a face like he said too much. Sucks in his lips as if trying to physically inhale the name he let escape his mouth.

I grab him by his shirt and lift him out of his chair. He barely weighs anything, he's as light as a stinky bag of feathers. "Who's Baxter?"

The darkness in Mac's eyes is now replaced worry.

"WHO . . . IS . . . BAXTER?"

Mac slowly brings a finger to his lips. Then points upward.

"Forget about the stupid rats! You've got bigger problems now."

The old man nods. "I know." He gestures for me to come closer. I hesitate, not sure what he's up to, but Mac squints at me . . . almost as if he's trying to communicate something. Reluctantly I bring my head close to his. He whispers in my ear, "He can hear us."

I pull back, shoot him a look. "Who?"

Mac leans close to my ear. "Baxter. I shouldn't have said his name, but it slipped. Actually, I said too darn much. Haven't had company in a while." He looks over Kylie like she's dessert. "Especially company so lovely. Maybe that's why I'm blabbering." His gaze drifts to the floor. "And now he's gonna kill me."

"No one is killing anyone else right now," I say loud enough so that this Baxter can hear me, too.

"Too late." Mac brings his hand up to cover my mouth, tears forming at the corners of his eyes—but I pull away, not sure what he's doing. He jumps up and down and makes flapping motions with his hands.

It's as if he's the only one playing charades.

"Grandpa's a damn nutcase." Chase cuts in between us, pushing us apart. "Shaman, psychic voodoo bullshit spells. Who gives a damn how we got here?" He points down at the floor. "I say we park our happy asses right here and wait until morning. I mean, you heard him. Those things can't come into the RV park."

Mac is full on jumping up and down, waving his arms like a madman.

"On second thought, maybe Grandpa's been stalling," Chase says as he leans close to Mac, sizing him up as if he wants to punch the old man out. Mac freezes. Glares back. "Maybe Grandpa here's been buying time for his boss to kill us himself. Especially since we've gotten this far and all."

Chase does make a good point.

"I said too much," Mac mumbles. "Said too damn much. But the game's going to change! It's OK. The game is already changing—"

"Shut up!" Chase stomps his foot to make the point that he's had enough.

"Chase!" I shout.

"Screw this nutjob." Chase turns to me. "Let's tie him to the chair and stay here until this whole thing blows over in the morning." To Mac, "Those things don't hunt during the day, do they?"

"The game's gonna change . . ." Mac mutters once more.

"Aw, come on, you worthless piece of shit." Chase shoves Mac, and the old man nearly falls over. "Answer me."

"Chase, stop it!" Kylie says, getting to her feet. "You're not helping!"

"Answer me!" Chase asks Mac once more. "They don't hunt during the day, do they? That's why we have to make it until morning, isn't that right?"

Mac goes stiff. "Yes . . . that's right. But you can't stay here until morning."

Kylie and I trade looks.

"Oh yeah?" Chase asks. "And why's that?"

Mac points down at the floor, then puts his hands together, then makes an exploding sound as he opens his hands.

"Cut the charades, Grandpa!" Chase mimics Mac's gestures as he asks, "What does that mean?"

"It means," I say, feeling a sudden chill run through me, "that this place is rigged with explosives."

Mac nods up and down.

The color drains from Chase's face.

"Stay. Leave. No matter what you decide to do, you'll all die tonight." A sneer stretches across Mac's weathered face. "Stay, and this place goes up in one gigantic mushroom cloud. Leave, and you all know who's waiting for you in the woods."

"And what if we keep heading east?" Kylie asks.

Mac looks over at her. "Well then, sweetie, you'll be traveling through the field of the dead."

"The what?" I ask.

"The field of the dead. The site where the Kenneh'wah village was that burned down. It's where the angriest of the tribe sleep. And I use the term sleep loosely." Mac wrinkles his nose as he flicks his tongue across his cavity-riddled teeth.

Chase goes white. An expression of pure dread is plastered all over his pasty skin. I see the wheels of fear turning in his head and share his sentiment.

"You guys are so dead," Mac says with a giggle. That twinkle of glee returning to his eyes. "You'll be recycled. Your soul will give way to theirs, and you'll be joining the ranks soon enough. Nothing more than fresh bodies for their age-old army."

I want to knock Mac out, but Chase beats me to it.

"Screw you, man!" Chase goes for Mac—but the old man moves surprisingly quick. Kicks Chase in the groin and pushes him back into me.

The two of us go tumbling onto the floor.

I hear Kylie shout, "Mac—stop!"

Mac just runs out of the trailer.

We get to our feet, move to the window.

Outside, Mac is sprinting surprisingly fast given his age and condition. He's waving his arms in the air as he heads straight for the forest.

"I'm one of you! Don't kill me!" he screams into the waiting darkness of the woods. "I'm not chek-tah! Don't kill me!"

"Should we go after him?" Chase asks.

"You mean, head back into those woods?" I shake my head. "No thank you."

"Good point."

Kylie asks, "Think he was telling the truth?"

"About what?"

"About the shaman? The bomb? I don't know . . . all of it?"

"After what we've been through tonight, I don't know what to believe. But we can't stay here. Explosives or no explosives."

Mac passes under the light pole at the outer edge of the RV camp.

Arms still up in the air, he's screaming that we're in the park, that we were holding him captive—

Something moves with the swiftness of a cheetah.

Runs right in front of Mac, wielding something in its hands.

Mac lets out a whimper, clutches his neck, drops to his knees, and then collapses, landing hard on the side of his head. The silhouette of a Kenneh'wah hunter stands above him. We watch as the hunter's eyes and teeth come to life, flickering like distant candles. He raises one arm, brandishing one of those bone knives, and screams out, "Chek-taaaaaaaah!"

"Jesus . . ." Chase says in a hoarse whisper. "They'll kill their own men."

"Mac wasn't one of their own," I say. "He's one of Baxter's. And to the Kenneh'wah, it seems that we're all chek-tah." I turn to Chase and Kylie as I say, "We're all invaders."

"OK, so now for the question of the evening, guys . . ." Kylie asks, "What do we do?"

"I say screw what that geriatric psycho said," Chase says, plopping himself down on the couch, "and let's camp our asses here for the night."

"You mean take our chances that Mac was bluffing?" I ask.

"As opposed to our alternative?" Chase points out the window. "Did you not just see him get his throat slit?"

"Oh my God . . ." Kylie says with a gasp. She's staring off toward the edge of the camp.

Mac is back on his feet again.

He turns toward the RV park, toward us, eyes and teeth aglow just like the other hunters. With both arms in the air, he lets out a raspy, "Chek-tah!" Then louder. "CHEK-TAAAAAAAAH!"

"It's a never-ending undead army from Hell," Kylie whispers under her breath, gaze fixed on the old man as he sways from side to side, drunk on whatever bloodlust is running through his reanimated veins.

With a nervous laugh, Chase adds, "Well he did say he was one of them . . . just before they offed him."

"How's this possible?" I ask, staring at Mac and his creepy glowing eyes.

"Does it matter? Not really," Chase says, still lounging on the chair like some cat, oblivious to the wild world outside. "All that matters is that Mac just made my case. Not only did he get killed, but the old raisin also came back as one of those Kenneh-whatever hunters."

"But if we stay here, and if what Mac said is true, we're dead for certain," I say, turning back to Chase and Kylie.

"Unless that's just a ploy to get us back out into the game," Kylie says. "What if Mac was bluffing?"

"Maybe, but then being that this sounds like Baxter's game, the man is probably not going to want to lose. And according to Mac, we did make it farther than anyone else has," I remind them. "Maybe Baxter gets pissed that we stayed the night in hotel RV here and flattens the camp out of frustration. Seems to be no shortage of those emotions here."

Outside Mac continues to chant check-tah as if taunting us to come out and face him.

"Rod, seriously. Wake up, man. If we go out there, we die. How much simpler can it be?" Chase hops to his feet, gestures outside toward Mac. "Look at him!"

Mac sways from side to side, screaming incoherently.

"He's just waiting for us out there."

"Yeah, I got it," I say. "So, we don't go that way."

Chase shrugs me off. "Oh? So where do we go then, genius?" He makes quotes with his fingers as he says in a mocking tone, "The field of the fucking dead?"

"Exactly," I say. "We keep heading east."

16

Human Radios & The Jumper

"That sounds like a terrible idea!" Chase turns to Kylie, a skeptical look on his face. "Don't tell me that you're thinking of going back out there, too?"

Kylie steps away from the window and glares at him.

"Sooooooo?" Chase gestures for her to spit out an answer.

"Being that Rodney didn't take off running, and you did . . ." She nods in my direction. "I'm sticking with him."

"Awwww, come on!" Chase throws his hands up in the air. "I ran because I was scared shitless."

Kylie folds her arms across her chest.

"Don't tell me you've never been afraid, princess. I'm sure you've got plenty of emotional instability yourself. Otherwise, you wouldn't be here. We've all got one thing in common, and apparently, it ain't a zest for living!"

"Slow your roll," Kylie says, holding a hand up.

"Uh-huh." Chase smirks. "You just made my point," he says as he glances down at the razor scars on her wrists.

She slaps Chase, knocking his head to one side.

Chase cups his cheek. "What the crap?" Opens and closes his jaw just to make sure it still works.

"How dare you judge me?" she says. "I'm sure you didn't grow up in a screwed up home like I did."

"Yeah, I did." Chase rubs his cheek.

"Oh? Really?" Kylie says. "Tell me about it."

Chase shrugs. Throws his hands in the air. "Yeah, my parents were super hard on me. Wanted me to get perfect grades. Make the soccer team. Get into Harvard or Yale." He chuckles, then says, "I settled for Columbia."

"And you just made my point," Kylie says. "Completely different childhoods." She leans forward, and Chase cringes, realizing his big mouth just opened a can of worms.

"My parents couldn't give a rat's ass if my sister, Casey, and I made it through middle school. In fact, my mom walked out on us by the time I had my first period. And not that you would understand this, since you're a guy, but going through puberty with an abusive asshole of a father sucked." She exhales deeply, closes her eyes for a moment as if reliving the pain. When she finally opens them, she tells us, "My father, Abe, was only good for two things: beating us and blaming us for Mom leaving."

"So," I ask cautiously, "why did your mom leave?"

"Because she couldn't handle that Casey and I were . . . special."

"Special?" Chase asks.

"We had these powers." She makes a face as she struggles to explain. "Powers as in the ability to express voices, thoughts, and even mimic gestures that weren't our own."

Chase raises an eyebrow. "You mean you guys were possessed?"

"More like receptive."

"That's a pretty way to put it," Chase says under his breath.

"We picked up on the energies of those who've passed and could channel them. Kind of like spiritual conduits, or as Casey used to call us, human radios." Kylie pauses, her gaze shifting between Chase and me. The muscles in her jaw tense as she goes on. "We provided the window and sometimes the microphone from their world back to ours."

"Umm . . . what does that even mean?" Chase asks.

"Chase!" I snap.

"What, Rod? It's an honest question."

"What are you? A cop?" My hands curl into fists.

"I'm just trying to understand, OK? This whole night has been a lot to digest," Chase says. "I mean we're being stalked by zombie hunters in a backwoods theme park overseen by a sadist. And now we find out that one of us is some sort of . . . clairvoyant?"

"I get it." I'm close to punching him. "But back off a little bit, all right?"

Chase eyes my fists. Nods as he backs down.

"Look, guys," Kylie says, "I get it, too. I know it's a lot to take in. And trust me . . . it's not something Casey or I asked to be born with, but we were. We had that ability. We could feel the presence of those who'd passed on and sometimes they would inhabit our bodies—if only for a minute, just to get a taste of our world again." Her gaze trails down to the floor, and a lock of her pink-and-blue hair spills across her brow. My hand twitches as I almost reach out to brush it aside, but I restrain myself.

The heck?

Why was I going to do that?

Why do I feel this connection with a woman I've known only a few hours?

Maybe it's just the stress of it all.

Some variant of Stockholm syndrome perhaps?

Kylie continues. "Our father really didn't appreciate this . . . gift. He called us 'little witches.' Told us that's why Mom left. She left because we were freaks." Her eyes glisten as she tears up. "And after many years of abuse and constant feelings of guilt, Casey finally broke. Took her life. Filled the bathtub, plugged in a toaster, and electrocuted herself." As the tears fall, her dark mascara runs. She bows her head and shakes it from side to side, sniffling as she whispers. "She got the idea from a movie." She lifts her head. "She was ten."

"Oh my God," I say. "I'm sorry."

"Losing someone you love, kind of does a number on you, you know? Never got over that. Probably never will." Kylie holds up her wrists, palms out. "And one day I'd had enough. Missed my sister too much. Hated myself for being a weirdo. Felt it was time to join her. So, I cut myself, but I didn't get too far. My roommate just happened to get home early from work. Saved me. Woo-hoo. Lucky me." She gets so close to Chase, it seems as though she's going to bite off his nose. "So . . . there you go. I tried to kill myself. Shocker."

Chase says nothing, his mouth slung open as if he suddenly lost all ability to speak.

"And yes, after a lifetime of pursuing affectionless relationships from non-committal pussies like you, I'm going to stick with Rodney because he and Bear have been the only men who haven't abandoned me when I needed them most." She laughs to herself. "Imagine that. Two strangers I met on a bus have been there for me more than any other man in my life."

Chase gulps. In a quivering tone, he asks, "Where-where-where is Bear?"

Kylie cocks her head to the side, somewhat bewildered. Studies him. It's as if Chase didn't hear a word she said.

"He didn't make it," I say.

Chase then asks Kylie, "Why didn't you mention that when you first saw me?"

"Because you never bothered to ask, you selfish jerk!" Kylie turns to me. "I'm ready to go when you are—"

"You're totally right, Kylie," Chase says.

Kylie looks back at him. "What?"

Chase slumps onto the couch, deflated. He stares at the floor as he says, "I'm a selfish jerk." He looks up at us as he goes on. "I'm also a stockbroker—was a stockbroker. Got heavy into day trading. Figured out a 'foolproof' system that worked for a while. Bought shit tons of stocks with other peoples' money, then unloaded them minutes later." He laughs to himself, gaze trailing back down to the ground.

"It's amazing what you can earn when your stock goes up just a few cents—pennies! Fucking pennies!"

Chase puts his head in his hands, and I glance over at Kylie. We share a moment, and I detect that she's as curious as I am about what's led the man here.

"Other peoples' pennies! And the easier the money came, the bigger my head got," Chase says as he lifts up his head. "I became addicted to the high of picking the right stocks. The high of winning. And the more money I made, the more my ego grew. And the more addicted I got, the more I pushed everyone away. I just wanted that high—that feeling of winning—to never go away. I would day trade in my sleep, during sex, while I was taking a shit. I literally could not stop thinking about the money. About the movement of pennies. About what stock I could snag at 9:30 a.m. the next day." He makes a gesture with his hands simulating an explosion. "Then it all blew up in my face. The market crashed. My system crumbled. And I lost everything. I lost my clients' money, then my own, then my job, and naturally anyone I had remotely cared about in my life I had already pushed away." He shrugs. "So I did what any irrational, desperate man would do."

I take a deep breath, knowing what's coming next.

"I tried to jump off a building. The very building I worked in." Tears form in Chase's eyes now. He looks at Kylie as he says, "I tried to kill myself for the very reasons you just spelled out."

Kylie says nothing. Crosses her arms again.

"I was disgusted with who I'd become. Who apparently I still am." He wipes away the tears quickly, not wanting to cry. "I'm really sorry for being that guy."

Kylie looks away.

"The only reason I didn't jump that day," Chase says as he dries off his eyes, "is because an old man with the wrinkled skin of a hundred-year-old prune showed up. He talked me out of jumping. Told me to start a new life. Said if I got down off the ledge and went to the bus station downtown there'd be a bus waiting for me. That it would lead me to my greater purpose." Eyes free of tears, he glances back up at us. "I thought that was a load of horseshit and told him to get lost until he said that he knew why I was going to kill myself. And he detailed how I was feeling right down to the last goddamn tear."

I feel my skin crawl as I put it together.

The shaman.

Chase points his thumb toward his chest and raises his voice a little as he continues. "And I never told anyone this shit! You guys are the first people to know."

"So how did he figure out your motivations for wanting to kill yourself?" Kylie asks.

Chase shrugs. "No clue. The moment I took my eyes off him to get down from the ledge, he vanished." He claps his hands together to drive the point home. "Poof! Old fart moved faster than a fucking ninja."

"So why'd you still go to the bus station?" I ask. "Why not just move on with life?"

"What life?" Chase snaps, tears brimming again. "I lost everything thanks to my own pride." He laughs at himself. "Figured if anyone knew that much about me and gave me some sort of direction—albeit random—it must've been a sign." He shakes. "Too bad it turned out to be a trick to get me into this trap."

"Or maybe it was a wake-up call in disguise," I say. "Maybe all of us needed tonight to see just how precious life is."

Chase wipes the tears away. "And maybe you should work for Hallmark."

"I'm not saying that we asked for this, Chase."

"Yeah, well maybe the old fart was right. Maybe we did ask for this."

The RV falls silent for a moment. I peek outside and find that Mac has vanished. There's no sign of the other hunters, either.

"Well, speaking of Mac," I say, breaking the silence. "He's gone. Probably a sign that we should get moving." Then to Chase, "So are you coming?"

Chase looks up at me, eyes red and puffy. A nice welt stretches across his face courtesy of Kylie's bitch slap—one he deserved for sure. "Yeah, let's do it. Screw it."

"At least now we've got a real weapon. One that won't disintegrate," I say as I pick up the shotgun. "And speaking of weapons, let's search the trailer for anything else we can use."

We spend the next few minutes ransacking the place, but only come up with six shotgun shells and two kitchen knives. Mac lived like a Spartan. Not much in the way of material possessions. Not even enough to cover his most basic needs, aside from bottled water and cans of sardines. It's no wonder he was going crazy, he was hiding out in an old trailer in the middle of nowhere, living off a diet of Marlboros and canned fish.

I throw open the front door and take a deep breath, not knowing what's ahead. Not knowing if leaving the RV is a mistake, but something about this park just doesn't feel safe. Not to mention feeling the constant anxiety of wondering if, at any moment, the place will go up in one big mushroom cloud.

I glance over my shoulder. Chase is clutching a butter knife in his hand. Kylie wields a long, sharp steak knife. The dried makeup smeared across her face now resembling a sort of war paint.

I hope I'm not leading us right into certain death.

17

Jump Right In

Outside it's dead quiet. Still no sign of Mac, Damien, or the rest of the hunting party. Though I'm sure they're watching. I wish their eyes would glow all the time, that way we would be able to see them coming. We cut through the park and push forward, continuing east. Up ahead, two light poles stream amber light down onto the outer edge of the camp. Beyond that lies the supposed field of the dead. I feel a little better knowing that all of us are armed this time around. Although my preference for weapons would've been more than kitchen utensils and only a handful of shotgun shells.

We pass under the warm yellow of the xenon bulbs above us, leaving the presumed safe border of the camp. It takes a moment for my eyes to once again adjust to the moonlight above as well as that ever-present red smog. I feel my stomach churn as we make our way deep into the forest. There's this tingling dread in my gut as if we're about to take a high dive, blindfolded, into a pool. No telling what to expect when we land.

Will the pool be empty? Or will a hundred hands be waiting to catch us and tear us apart?

The only certainty is uncertainty.

"Keep moving," I tell Kylie and Chase, but I say this to myself as well. Don't want to let fear get the best of me or slow me down. Besides, it's a little late for that. To let panic take over means death, and I'm not about to give these maniacs the pleasure.

We run for a while, cutting through the thick foliage as fast as our legs, lungs, and hearts will allow. I'm starting to wonder where this field is when we spot a break in the forest up ahead. We hop through the last wall of bushes and shrubs and come upon a vast meadow. The celestial bodies above rain down milky white light, uninterrupted by the dense canopies of cypress, magnolia, and oak that comprise most the wooded areas around here.

The only trees in the middle of the field ahead are leafless, with twisting branches that reach up into the night sky like giant, skeletal hands. The ground is covered in a sea of three-foot-tall grass, glowing as if strands of red rope-lights were strewn about at our feet. Just above the blades of grass, a thousand flickering lights come to life, each one alternating colors of yellow and white.

My first thought is that since we made our way to the plot of the Kenneh'wah's former village, a mob of very pissed-off hunters has just awoken to defend it. But I quickly realize that these aren't the eyes of the tribe. They're—

"Fireflies?" Chase says in a hoarse whisper.

"Yeah," Kylie whispers back. "And they kind of just showed up out of nowhere and for no reason."

"Maybe we disturbed them," Chase says.

"You might actually be right." I glance at Chase, then Kylie. "I bet it's a signal to the Kenneh'wah."

"A signal?" she asks, staring out at the field, at the swarming cloud of brilliant, floating stars. "How do you know that?"

"Just a guess." I feel my stomach churn once more as I say, "Though something tells me that they know we're here."

Chase curses and stomps his foot. "I already regret not staying in the RV!"

Behind us, from the belly of the forest—the very direction we just came from—a loud bang, followed by the sound of several explosions. We drop to the ground as a wave of hot air rushes over our bodies. I think Kylie screamed, but the deafening sound momentarily drowns out everything. We roll onto our backs in time to see a great mushroom cloud swirl upward into the sky. Its source?

West.

Where the RV park is . . .

Or was.

Mac was right. The RV park was rigged after all. I get a slight sense of peace knowing that I made the right decision getting us out of there. But that peace is quickly replaced by the reality that we are still not free yet. Seems Baxter is very much in tune with what goes on in his arena of death here.

We watch in silence as the curling ball of fire and smoke unravels into the night.

"OK, so maybe that crazy prick was telling the truth after all," Chase says. From the corner of my eye, I catch him glance at me. "Thanks."

"Thank me when we're all drinking mojitos on South Beach."

We get to our feet. Up ahead the fireflies continue their creepy dance, twirling and zigzagging haphazardly over the field. A thought pops into my brain—under different circumstances this would be a truly spectacular sight. One to enjoy while sitting on the hood of a car, a bottle of wine on my left, and my woman on my right...

A flare rockets up in the sky just beyond the field. East.

"My God," Kylie says with a gasp. "It's like Baxter is watching our every move." I turn in time to see the twinkle of the dying flare reflected in her eyes as her gaze follows it. She snaps her head in my direction, catches me staring at her. "What?"

Clearing my throat, I answer her with, "Nothing. I just had a thought."

That, under different circumstances, I would totally ask you out on a date.

That I would be so lucky to have someone as courageous, stunning and strong as you by my side...

Gazing at fireflies dancing above the tall grass as we sip wine—

Shaking off those random, stupid thoughts, I tell her the next thing that comes to mind: "Baxter wants to see how far we'll get." Her eyes meet mine. "He's probably hunkered down somewhere, staring at a dozen monitors. Jerking off. Somewhat titillated at the possibility that we might actually make to the finish line."

Chase scoffs. "If there is one."

"I think there is," I say. "And we're going to find it here real soon."

"But what makes you so sure?" Kylie asks me.

"Because we've made it this far." I glance out into the field, gripping my shotgun as if it's my best friend right now—because it is—and I turn back to them. "You guys ready?"

They both nod.

"I'll lead. Stay close to me. Kylie, you watch our sides. Chase, you take the rear."

"Oh sure. Make the guy with the butter knife the caboose!" Chase whines, holding up the knife. "Come one, man. I'm sure you've seen enough movies to know the last one in line is the first one to get picked off."

"I don't think the Kenneh'wah have watched enough movies to know that."

"Yeah, but I'm sure Damien has."

Without further discussion, I pat his shoulder and say, "There's only three of us left. So please cover the rear."

"Fine!" he says in a huff.

"Kylie, you keep one hand on my shoulder. Chase, you keep a hand on Kylie's shoulder. This way, we stay close and avoid getting split up. We're going to move quick, but steady."

"Aaaaaand why don't we just haul ass?" Chase asks.

"I don't know about you guys, but between the adrenaline, the running, and the fighting, I'm beyond wiped. Which is a bit of an understatement. Not to mention we haven't eaten." I glance toward the field, at the swirling fireflies, and then turn back to the group. "We need to conserve as much energy as we can in case we get ambushed out there."

"And what if they show up and just start shooting arrows at us?" Kylie asks.

"Well . . . then we haul ass."

"Oh, great plan," Chase says as he rolls his head backward.

"It's the only one I've got." I take another deep breath as if I'm going to jump out of an airplane, and say, "Let's go."

18

The SWAT Drill

We hop over a small bank of shrubs and enter the field. The three of us look as though we're doing some sort of a bizarre SWAT drill. I'm leading. Kylie's behind me, hand clenching my shoulder tight. Chase is hopefully keeping at least one hand on her. My shotgun is at eye level. The stock is pressed tight against my shoulder. The front sight alternating between two o'clock and ten o'clock. With only six shots, I'll have to make them count.

The silence is almost deafening. Nothing stirs, nothing moves save for the swirling cloud of harmless luminescent bugs flying around us and the gentle sway of the tall grass in the thick humid air. Between the moon, stars and the red fog, it's almost so bright out you'd think it was dawn.

Wish it was.

We press on. Walking through this grass is like wading through water. The field is the length of maybe two football fields. Surprisingly we're already almost halfway through it.

The further across the field we get, the more I start to worry.

This is too easy.

It's too quiet.

No war cries.

No mutterings of "Chek-tah."

Just the crunching of grass in our wake and the sounds of our own rapid breathing.

"You guys good?" I ask in a whisper loud enough for them to hear.

"Yeah," Kylie answers with an exasperated huff.

"Chase?"

"I'm fantastic."

"You see anything back there?" I ask him.

"Just a bunch of flying night lights."

"Great. Keep up this pace," I say as we continue forward. "We're almost there, guys." With our tight little formation, we'll catch sight of them no matter which direction they come from.

"Good. My leg's starting to cramp," Chase complains just above a whisper. "Walking backward is a pain in the ass."

"At least we're still walking," Kylie snaps.

"True." With a bit of a laugh, Chase says, "Remind me to join a gym when I get to Miami—"

Chase screams out in pain.

I hear fumbling noises behind me. Kylie lets go of my shoulder, and I spin around to find her rushing to his aid.

"Something's got me! Something's got my leg!" Chase struggles with some invisible force hidden within the grass.

Kylie reaches over and tries to pull Chase up—when she goes down, too.

"Kylie!" I reach out, grab her by the arm and pull, but she doesn't budge. Feels like she's anchored to the ground.

"What the fuck? WHAT THE FUCK?!" Chase screams as he stabs downward with the butter knife. "Get off me!"

Kylie slips out of my grip as something yanks her away from me, dragging her into the grass, where she disappears.

"Rodney!" Kylie cries out, and then the next time she shouts my name, it's somewhat muffled. I drop to my knees and cut a path in the grass with my hands. I catch Kylie's shoes kicking and scraping against the ground. Something has got her pinned.

"Kylie!" I nearly dive on top of her. Indeed, she's stuck. Two rotten arms with skin that is blackened and peeling like overcooked meat hold her against the ground. It's as if the earth suddenly grew a pair of arms and reached out for the closest thing it could for a hug. One of the rotten arms is wrapped around Kylie's torso, hand clenched around her face, practically suffocating her. The other is wrapped around her waist, fingers digging into her skin.

I try to pry the arms off her, but they're holding on to her as if she's a treasure that they're not willing to part with. I jump to my feet, take the butt of the shotgun and whack at the arm around her waist. It recoils, and the other arm loosens, allowing me to grab Kylie's hand, pull her free and bring her back to her feet.

"You OK?" I ask, breathlessly.

Before she can answer, the owner of those decayed arms emerges from the ground, rising like a snake, lumps of earth sloughing off its body. Its head is a dirt-caked skull with glowing teeth. It lets out a guttural howl as it reaches for her—but not before I knock her aside and ram the butt of the shotgun into its chin, breaking it off as though it were a chunk of ice. It responds with a screech, then charges at me, but doesn't get far as I jam the shotgun butt so hard against its skull, I knock it clean off its torso.

"RODNEY! KYLIE!" Chase screams out. "SOMEBODY HELLLLLP!"

Both Kylie and I spin in circles, looking for any sign of Chase in this sea of grass. He's nowhere to be found, but he's got to be close. Got to be right next to us.

"Chase!" I shout. "CHASE!"

"OVER HERE, DAMMIT!"

We scan the field, but still no sign of him.

"Where?" I shout.

Then I see Chase kick a foot up in the air. The tip of his shoe sailing up above the grass just long enough for us to see where exactly he's at. Whatever grabbed him dragged him a good thirty feet from us. Both Kylie and I break into a sprint, moving as fast as we can through the thick grass.

"HURRY THE HELL UP!"

It's the one time I'm glad to hear Chase's voice. We finally stumble upon him, and he's in a worse situation than Kylie. One of those zombie things is on top of him, snapping its jaws at his face. The clacking sound of its jagged, rotten teeth trying to snap off a chunk of his face sends a shiver through my core. Before it gets another chance to bite, I whack the thing's skull with the shotgun, knocking it off Chase and onto the ground.

The thing recovers, hisses at me. Its empty eye sockets bore into me with malevolence. It springs to its feet with surprising speed and is about to pounce on me when the blast from my shotgun splits its head open. Dust and bone explode in all directions. The odor is horrible. The stench of steam, sulfur, and rot nearly chokes me.

Kylie gets Chase to his feet. He's clutching the side of his neck. Blood seeping down his shirt.

"Oh God," she says under her breath. "You're bleeding."

"That thing scratched me."

"That's more than a scratch," I say as I try to move his hand away from the wound, but he swats it.

"OK . . . it bit me, all right? Bit the shit out of me then dragged me halfway across the world. Like, fast. Super-fucking fast." Chase clutches the side of his neck even tighter. "I think it was planning on chomping me to death."

"You OK though?" Kylie asks.

Chase nods. "I'm a little woozy, and this hurts like a bitch, but other than that, I'll be okay. Especially once my happy ass gets to a hospital in Miami."

I shoot him a look. Something doesn't feel right.

"What?" Chase asks. "Am I not allowed to get injured?"

Before I can answer that, moans echo through the field. Dark shadows emerge from all directions behind us, floating up from the depths of the ocean of grass like icebergs appearing in the night.

"Rodney?" Kylie tugs at my shirt.

The entire field of the dead has just shown up to welcome us.

"Hmm . . . I think that's our sign," Chase says with a nod. "We should run."

"Right. Let's move." I turn and start for the eastern edge of the field. "Come on!"

And we're running. I glance over my shoulder. At least a hundred of those things are marching after us. The thought of them munching on us for dinner sends shivers through me.

Mental note: don't look back anymore.

Kylie and Chase's ragged breathing tells me they're just as tired as I am.

"Keep going!" I say between breaths. "We're almost there."

The groan of the swarm of dead behind us draws closer, evolving into more of a roar. I want to look back, to see how close they are, but I resist. We're almost there. Feels like the edge of the field is miles away, but it's only a few more feet.

I'm hoping that once we make it off the field and into the forest ahead, we either lose them or by some magical power, they stop chasing us. Maybe they're limited to the confines of that field. That would only make sense since it is called the field of the dead. Then again, seems we've been chased by the dead all night.

Difficult to tell what to believe anymore.

The moans behind us are so close I swear I can feel their breath on the back of my neck. But that's just my nerves and an anticipation of being bitten that's getting the best of me.

"Keep going!" I shout that more for myself than them this time.

Almost . . .

There . . .

All at once we burst through the eastern edge of the grass wall, bolt across a small clearing, and make it into the forest.

My legs burn. Can't help but come to a stop. I keel over, heaving. "Guys . . . let's . . ." Talking is beyond difficult right now. "Take a second . . ." Even though there's no guarantee that the undead army is taking a breather themselves, I just can't run anymore.

I draw in as much air as my lungs can handle and I'm met with the eerie silence of crickets . . .

And nothing else.

I spin around.

The zombie army has vanished, seemingly disappearing back down into the tall grass from which they came.

But not only have they vanished.

So have Chase and Kylie.

Oh God, no!

Did they get them? Or did I just outrun them?

I make my way back toward the field and stop short of where the tall grass begins again. I'm about to call out for them, when I hear Kylie scream, "RODNEEEEEEY!"

Her cries come, not from out there on the field but behind me.

Deep within the forest. I whirl around and hear her cry out from the belly of the woods again.

"Kylie!"

I make a dash in the direction of her voice.

She screams for me once more.

I cut between the trees, driven by a fire in my blood that pushes me through the exhaustion and burning of my muscles. I run so fast I nearly trip over my own feet, but after a few minutes, I find Kylie sprawled out on the ground. A gash on her forehead. She's bleeding like crazy.

"Please, God, no!" I drop to my knees, and I'm about to lift her up when a voice behind me says:

"Chek-taaaaaaah!"

I turn in time to see Chase standing above me. His eyes aglow, teeth pulsing like rows of tea lights. That nasty wound in his neck, that ugly bite, now fully exposed. It was more than just a scratch.

A third of his neck is missing.

And he's holding a sturdy tree branch. "Chek-tah!"

Before I can get to my feet, he swings.

The last thing I feel before everything goes dark is the crunching of wood against my jaw.

19

Joining the Ranks

I awaken to treetops and a starlit sky sparkling like a million tiny diamonds. Welcome back to the night that just never seems to end.

The treetops start to slide past my view. Leaves crackling all around me.

I'm being dragged.

I lift up my head. Chase pulls me by my feet with one hand, carries my shotgun in the other. My feet are bound with a rudimentary rope; thin twigs snaked around each other. Surprisingly it's sturdy enough to bind my feet.

Up ahead, one of the hunters drags Kylie by her ankles.

"Chase, what are you doing?" I ask.

Chase glances over his shoulder. That unnerving glow coming to life in his eye as he says, "Taking you to Damien."

"What? Why?"

"So he can scalp you . . . himself."

Chase runs me over a rock that carves a path up my spine and clips the base of my skull. I wince, white-hot pain radiating throughout my head.

"Sorry." Chase laughs. "Not sorry."

"Why?" I ask as the pain subsides. "Are you helping them?"

Chase and the hunter stop abruptly. He turns to face me, still clutching my feet in an unnaturally strong grip. The river of blood cascading down Chase's torso gleams in the moonlight like some bizarre, bloody necktie. His newfound physique outlined by the red haze. Seems after death, or whatever this transition is, he's become more fit, brandishing the body of an athlete and not a cubicle-bound stockbroker.

"Because I'm one of the Kenneh'wah now." Chase's eyes flicker a yellowish-red. "And this is the best thing that could've happened to me." He inhales deeply as if breathing in oxygen for the first time. "I mean, look at me." He flexes his free arm. Bicep bulging. "I'm ripped as a beast and didn't have to sling around weights to get this way."

"They did something to you."

"Yeah, they did. They made me stronger through death." His eyes pulse. "Their death. Their transformation. I'm becoming one of them. I feel their hate pumping through my veins."

"Is that what you want, Chase?"

"Fuck yeah, it is." He bares his teeth, and they spark to life. "To no longer feel lost, depressed, or unworthy. I've got a sense of purpose now. A mission."

"Really? What's that?"

"To kill chek-tah like you." And with a hard yank, he continues, dragging me toward wherever we're headed. The hunter does the same. "I feel sorry for Liza and the others. They didn't transition quite so well into a Kenneh'wah warrior. Weak souls. Mindless ghouls best suited for the field of the dead. Not me. I'm a fighter."

"A fighter? I distinctly remember you running off at one point."

"Just looking out for myself, as I always have."

Chase may have taken my shotgun, but he didn't get all my weapons. He also made a mistake not tying up my hands. I reach into my pocket, retrieving what I hope is my pocket knife and not one of the shotgun shells. It's the knife. I pop it open, hoist myself up in one desperate movement, and jam the blade in-between his knuckles. He lets out a wild howl and drops my feet.

Chase yanks the pocket knife from his hand. Eyes it with contempt.

"What the fuck?"

I make quick work of breaking the twig ropes off my feet. The other hunter drops Kylie and moves toward me, but I drive my heel right into his shin. He cries out and tumbles to the ground.

"Oh no you don't!" Chase fumbles with the shotgun.

Too late.

I'm already at his side.

I wrap my arms over Chase's firing arm, directing the barrel of the shotgun at the other hunter just as he pulls the trigger.

The hunter takes the brunt of the blast. His gray flesh exploding as the round tears open his midsection. He goes down quick.

Before Chase can react, I elbow him in the nose. He stumbles backward, releasing his grip on the shotgun. I yank it away, spin on my heels, and pull the trigger just as Chase charges into me. He knocks the barrel aside as the shotgun roars. The shot completely misses. He takes me down the ground, landing on top of me with the force of a falling boulder. He weighs more than I expect, but then again, he isn't exactly Chase.

He's something else.

Chase straddles me and pins me down. With one hand, he grips my throat so tight I see spots. With the other, he holds up my pocket knife. Glares at it with a sneer. "You think this little toy was going to stop me? Are you kidding? A fucking spork is sharper than this!" He leans forward, his body weight cutting off circulation to my head. "How about I carve out both of your eyes with it?"

I try desperately to pry him off, but can't. It's as if he's made of concrete.

"I think I'll start with your left eye." He brings the slender blade up to my eyelashes. I flinch and try to turn away—but now he slides the hand he was choking me with up to my face. His thumb digs just under my cheekbone, locking me painfully in place. Fingernails cutting into skin. His grimy palm completely covers my nose and mouth. It's nearly impossible to breathe, and that's made even worse by the stench of his skin. He smells like sewage.

"The last thing you're going to see before I dig out your eyes is my smiling face," Chase says, teeth aglow.

I squeeze my eyes shut. Mentally preparing myself for the pain. But instead of experiencing the horrific sensation of a sliver of metal being shoved into my eye socket, I feel Chase loosen his grip around my face. Followed by the sounds of gagging.

I open my eyes.

Kylie!

She's standing behind Chase. A bone knife protrudes from his neck. Mouth open, tongue dangling out like some crazed canine. His face is frozen in a moment of surprise. The light in his teeth and eyes fades to black.

Kylie retrieves the bone knife and kicks Chase's lifeless body aside.

"Where'd you get that?" I ask, eyeing the weapon.

She extends her hand and pulls me to my feet. "From Chase's buddy over there." She nods toward the dead hunter.

"Well, you're a resourceful one."

She smiles in a way that says, I know. The wound at her temple is still bleeding.

"Your head. It looks—" I move to touch it, and she shrinks back.

"I'm all right."

"Yeah, I've heard that before," I say as I eye Chase's body.

"Don't worry, Rodney. Nothing bit me. That asshole simply clubbed me good with a branch back there."

The dull ache in my skull reminds me of a similar encounter.

"Well..."

Her eyes meet mine. "Well, what?"

"Thanks."

"For?" Kylie wipes the blood off on her shirt and then stuffs the knife through her belt.

"For saving my ass." I pick up the shotgun.

She laughs.

"What so funny?" I ask.

"We're not out of the woods yet."

I wince at the cliché, then grin.

"Sorry, I had to," she says with a smile herself.

"So . . ." The words that follow seem to come out of my mouth on their own. "If we make it out of this alive, can I take you out sometime?"

Kylie hesitates. It's almost as if she hadn't heard me correctly.

I feel the color drain from my entire body.

Why did I just ask that?

Could it be the shock of the situation? Adrenaline? Testosterone? Stupidity?

Kylie approaches me, comes very close to my body, and I lock up. I nearly jump when she gently places both hands on my shoulders. Her touch feels electric. I swear I can feel the energy jumping off her skin as if she's some sort of cosmic generator creating an attraction greater than the forces that keep our planets in orbit.

I wonder if she feels it, too.

"We will make it out of this alive. Count on that." Her words are like gold to my ears. I hope what will follow will be a yes to my question. "And as far as you taking me out—"

A flare shoots up in the air.

It's close.

"Look!" she says, pointing toward it. "Just beyond those trees." She squints. "Check out the lights up ahead."

War cries stir behind us.

"Come on," I say, pulling her in the direction of the flare. "It's time to finish this."

20

The Struggle and the Game

Gathering up every bit of energy in our bodies, we sprint through the last stretch of woods. Behind us, a stampede of undead hatred pursues us. Their war cries and footfalls sound as though they're literally right behind us. This time, I dare not look back. Instead, I keep my eyes on the lights up ahead.

We break through the woods and find ourselves in an RV park that's smaller than the one where we encountered Mac. There are only two RVs here. And just like Mac's park, these are encircled by a ring of light poles. Must be another "safe zone."

As we cross the small field and make our way to the first RV, the cries of the Kenneh'wah hunters grows deafeningly loud. Still, we march forward. My shotgun is raised and ready.

"Rodney, look!" Kylie points to the woods.

Once more, a wall of warriors lines up shoulder to shoulder along the edge of the forest, stopping short of the perimeter of the camp as if there's some invisible barrier holding them back. They're yelling, making faces, and pumping fists and weapons in the air. Their bodies sway from left to right, seemingly drunk on the primordial passions of their unresolved loathing.

At the center of the group—Damien. He's ripped off the flap of flesh from his scalp, giving us a clean view of the pale, milky gray of the top of his skull. "Aaaaaand where do you all think you're going?"

he asks, folding his arms.

"As far away from here as possible!" Kylie shouts back.

"You naive bitch." Damien's shoulders bounce as he laughs. "Do you really think there's a pot of gold at the end of this rainbow?"

I tug Kylie by the arm, gesturing that we need to keep moving. To not pay Damien the attention he's goading for.

He wants to feed our fears.

To remind us that they're tracking us like a pack of wolves.

Damien then asks Kylie, "Are you that stupid to think that those flares are leading you to freedom?"

"Guess we'll find out!" Kylie yells.

Damien exchanges glances with his fellow undead.

"Come on. Let's go," I tell Kylie. "He's just pissed because he can't get us."

"That's right, you pussies. Run!" Damien sneers. "You'll be back soon enough! And I'll be waiting. Especially for you, Rodney boy!"

"You won't have the pleasure!" I shout back.

"Oh really?" Damien says, with one eyebrow raised. "Uh oh." His eyes suddenly widen as he points at me . . . or rather past me. "Better look behind you."

A shiver of nerves runs down my body as I turn around . . . and I'm cracked across the face with something fast and hard.

Vaguely, I hear Kylie shouting as my body hits the grou—

***

I awaken to the pungent smell of cigarette smoke and find myself inside a trailer. My first thought is that I'm somehow back in Mac's RV. But as things come into focus, instead of Mac, I see a heavyset man in a wheelchair. He's balding with a few white strands neatly combed over the crown of his head. He's got a massively round and swollen nose, marred with gin blossoms, no doubt from seeing the bottom of too many bottles over the years. To his left stands Jim

Grimm, indifferent and expressionless, with a shotgun in hand.

"My name's Baxter Neeley," the heavyset man says as he fires up a cigarette. "I'm sure that name should ring somewhat of a bell, Rodney."

"How do you know my name?"

"Oh, a little old magic man told me."

The throbbing in my head is quickly evolving into a migraine, it's so severe I feel nauseous. I try to bring my hands to my head, but can't because they're handcuffed to my chair.

"Sorry about that," Baxter says, eyeing my cuffs. "I've never had anyone make it this far . . . without me allowing it. So that tells me you're either lucky or somewhat of a fighter. Neither of which I want to take a chance on."

I scan the room. It's just the three of us.

"Where's Kylie?" I ask.

"Your friend's fine." He nods toward one of the doors in the room. "She's . . . resting."

"Resting?" I try to jump up, but the handcuffs restrain me. Jim takes a step forward with the shotgun, but Baxter gestures for him to back down.

"Trust me. She's OK," Baxter says as the cigarette flops up and down in his mouth.

"Trust you?" I repeat. "You're a murderer."

"I just don't understand." Baxter leans back in his wheelchair and takes a deep breath. Shakes his head in confusion. "I thought you people wanted to end your lives. Now suddenly, you all want to live? Why? Because the choice was taken out of your hands?"

I'm racking my brain for a way out of this. How to get out of these stupid handcuffs? Still, even if I did, Jim would blow me away before I could get my butt off this chair.

"Have you ever taken the time to think past your own selfishness?" Baxter asks me. "Taken a chance to think of all those folks who have died in car accidents, robberies, random shootings, plane crashes, and hospital beds? You think they got a choice? How selfish of any of you to believe you're any different." Baxter wheels himself over to a bottle of gin awaiting him on a weathered poker table.

"And who says you get to play God?" I ask. "Who says you get to decide who lives or dies?"

Baxter cocks his head to the side, takes a drag from his cigarette, and blows smoke straight up in the air like a chimney. He sighs, closes his eyes, and then reopens them, shifting his gaze to me with the look of a man who's tired of explaining himself. "I get to play God because I can do whatever I want." He smacks his thigh. "God took use of my legs. Allowed a drunk driver to crash into me while I was stopped at a red light." Anger flashes in his eyes. His mouth curls into a snarl as he recounts his story. "That drunk driver was looking to end his life. Well, he did—at my expense. And when he died, he took use of my legs and half of my body with him. Left me impotent. Less of a man." He looks down at the floor. "Didn't take long for my bitch of a wife to leave me for someone else." He pounds the poker table, and the bottle of gin does a little hop. "So I figure now God owes me one. He has to take a backseat while I get a little payback."

"And killing innocent people is going to bring back the use of your dick?"

"Innocent?" Baxter laughs. "Who's innocent?" He leans forward. "Last I checked, suicide is a ticket straight to Hell."

"You're the last person in the world who gets to preach about what's right and what's wrong."

"The way I see it, I saved you. I saved you all." Baxter takes another drag and then crushes out his cigarette. "If it weren't for me, you'd all be in Heaven's basement. Souls permanently set to broil in the Devil's oven."

"What are you talking about?"

"I'm talking about being your savior. You think it was pure chance that you escaped killing yourself? I am in touch with potent magic, or rather a magician of sorts. A shaman. And he is the one who saved you from an eternal afterlife in Hell and gave you a chance to be reborn into an army of purity."

I shake my head. "I find it hard to believe a monster like you has a concept of Heaven and Hell. Of right and wrong."

"Everyone gets their jollies off somehow." Baxter pours himself a drink. "Alcohol. Drugs. Porn. Gambling." He downs the shot. "Me? I just like watching people die." He waves his index finger in the air. "That's why I have hundreds of Wi-Fi cameras strung up in the trees."

"You sick bastard!" If only I could break out of these restraints, I'd beat the shit out of this monster and his sidekick.

Baxter takes a drag of his cigarette, blows a puffy gray cloud in my direction. Studies me for a moment, then says to Jim, "Send this asshole back out there." He unlocks my cuffs, then spins his wheelchair around to face Jim. "He's not done playing the game."

"Gladly." Jim brings the shotgun up to my face. "You heard the man." He nods toward the door. "Get off your ass, keep those hands up, and move!"

As anger ferments in my gut, I ask Baxter, "This isn't a game, is it?"

With an inquisitive look, he asks, "What exactly do you mean by that?"

"By definition, a game would imply that there's a chance one of the players might win." With a scoff, I say, "But we're not meant to win this, are we?"

Baxter freezes in place. On his face, first a look of contempt, and then curiosity. "Actually, somebody always wins." He takes one last puff of his cigarette and serves himself another shot. "And that somebody is me."

"You know what I'd like to know?"

"Indeed . . ." Baxter is about to down the shot, but pauses. He lowers the glass. "I would."

"Just how long you'd last out there." I gesture toward the woods.

"Guess you'll never know." Baxter pounds the shot and slams the glass on the table. "Now get out of my face!"

Jim jabs me in the ribs with the shotgun, and I nearly keel over. "Move it, chief!" He escorts me toward the door, but I stop short.

Through gritted teeth, clutching my side, I mutter, "This game's about to change. I promise."

With a huff, Baxter says, "You shouldn't make promises you know you can't keep."

"Don't worry," I say. "I don't."

Jim prods me again with the shotgun.

I take a pained breath, grunting as the air fills my lungs and swells my ribcage. As I push open the door, I mumble to Jim, "You're part of this game, too."

"Yeah, but I'm on the winning team. Now move your ass!"

21

The Long Walk

Outside, Jim ushers me back toward the woods, toward the edge of the camp. Surprisingly the Kenneh'wah have all vanished. Although I'm sure they're somewhere. Waiting and watching from the shadows. Damien right alongside them. Gushing for the chance to kill me. But before we get very far, I hear Baxter call out, "Jim! Wait!"

Jim frowns, then mumbles to me, "Stay put, chief." This is followed by another painful jab at my backside with his shotgun. To Baxter, he says a very annoyed, "Yeah...? What's up?"

"You know . . . Rodney's right!"

"About?" Jim answers, the word sounding more like a groan than a response.

"Well, it's not a game unless one side has the chance to win."

"So what? That's never mattered before."

"Correct, but then no one's ever gotten this far before either, James."

"It's Jim, goddammit. You know I hate when you call me that."

Baxter laughs. "Yeah. I know." Then he says, "So, Rodney..."

I say nothing. Keeping my eyes on the glowing forest ahead.

"Come on, Rodney. Turn around and face me! Don't be rude."

Reluctantly I do as asked and find Baxter parked on the porch of his trailer, gin bottle in one hand, ever-present shot glass in the other.

"Now since you made it this far, I'm willing to reward your survival skills," Baxter says. "Your newfound will to live."

"Reward me?" And now I feel like I'm talking to Satan himself. What kind of bargaining does the Devil do?

"Let's be honest. You and the woman have shown some miraculous resilience. Frankly, I'm in awe that you're both still alive. Be a shame to kill you so quickly. That'd be no fun after all." He pours himself another shot. "I rather enjoy the challenge. Your survival has proven very refreshing after too many years of folks easily being slaughtered like cattle to my native friends here. Don't quite think they had the same will to live as you two have shown."

The more I hear him talk, the more I grow to hate this man. "Get to your point."

"The point is, I'm willing to let one of you go as a reward for making it to the finish line." He throws back his head and gulps down the gin.

"It's not a finish line if one of us is still in the game."

"Let's clarify things, Rodney. It's my game. I can do whatever I want!" he says, slamming down the shot glass. "Take it or leave it. Your choice. You leave, or the woman leaves."

The psychotic entertainment never ends in Baxter's world. He's the Goldilocks of dungeon masters. Seems he doesn't want his "players" to die so quickly, but at the same time, refuses to let them win outright.

He wants everything to be just right.

To be perfectly balanced in his twisted, little mind.

Baxter continues. "And Jim here will personally take whomever you choose out of here and straight to Miami. Isn't that right?"

"I . . . will?" Jim asks with a bit of surprise in his voice.

"Yes, you certainly will."

"And what happens to the other person?" I ask. "To the one who remains."

"Well, what do you think?" Baxter pours another shot and then brings the glass to his lips as he says, "It's back to the playing field."

He downs the shot.

Back to the playing field?

To an untamed woodland full of undead monsters?

No, I can't let Kylie go back. A dozen vicious Kenneh'wah with anger issues against one, albeit tough, woman are lousy odds. Not to mention I'm sure that Damien would love to have his way with her.

Yeah, no way. I'd rather go in her place. Even if I don't make it out of those woods alive, I'd still rather take the fall than let her. Besides . . .

I almost took a bullet from my own gun and died for the wrong woman.

I'm more than happy to take an arrow and die for the right one.

"So you or her?" Baxter's raspy voice snaps me out of thought.

"I'll stay. Kylie can go free."

"If I may ask . . . why?"

"A hundred reasons. For starters, I'm not leaving her here for you guys to have fun with."

Baxter raises an eyebrow. "What makes you so sure we won't have fun with her . . . after you're dead?"

I move forward like I'm going to take his head off, but Jim promptly raises the shotgun. "Easy there, chief," he says. "Save that fight for them natives."

Baxter waves, smiling wide. "Don't worry . . . I won't touch her."

Jim chuckles. Then gestures for me to turn back toward the trees.

Baxter shouts, "If it's any consolation, you've been a real treat to watch."

Oh, the things I would do to Baxter if given half a chance.

But that won't be happening anytime soon.

In just a few minutes, I'll be back in the Kenneh'wah theme park. Weaponless. Tired. And the only target of Damien's loathing.

"Keep those hands up and keep walking," Jim says.

The closer we get to the edge of camp, toward the enveloping quiet darkness of the trees where the hunters are waiting for me, the more

I feel like a prisoner marching down a hallway toward death row.

I can't help but ask, "Why are you doing this?"

"Doing what?" Jim snaps, my question catching him off guard.

"Why are you helping that asshole?"

"Because that asshole pays me well."

"That really it?"

Jim says nothing and my ears are filled with only the soft sounds of our feet crushing dried grass. We're almost to the edge of camp and the closer we get, the brighter the red glow emanating from the woods gets. It's as if Baxter's cursed playing field senses my presence as I approach—

Perhaps that's it.

Perhaps the ground is alive—or, rather, dead.

Jim breaks the silence. "Baxter saved my life."

"You mean he spared you from the Kenneh'wah?" I ask. "Spared you from getting ripped to shreds."

"Now what makes you say that?"

"Back on the bus, you showed us your scars, suggesting that you had survived," I say. "You implied that you had made it through the night."

"So?"

"Baxter said Kylie and I were the first to make it as far as we did."

Jim lets out a throaty laugh followed by a sigh. "You're a hell of a good listener, chief."

"You're a lousy liar."

"So I lied about surviving the game," he says. "So what? But I didn't make that up about Baxter saving my life. I was one click away from blowing off the top of my head with this very shotgun. Thankfully that shaman picked up on my vibe, directed me toward Baxter's game."

"How exactly did he do that?" I ask.

"I had dreams about a bus, a bus that took me to freedom," he says. "There was an old man in the dream. He had long gray hair. Tan, wrinkled skin. He spoke in a language I'd never heard, yet I could understand him completely. Told me the bus would take me to a man in a wheelchair. This man would give me a new life. A new purpose."

As we make our way closer to the edge of camp, I glance up to see several clouds blocking out the moon. For the moment, the only thing illuminating our path is the glowing red forest ahead and the dim yellow light casting down from the light poles outlining the perimeter of Baxter's camp.

Jim continues. "That man—who I would later come to know as Baxter—felt my desperation. My desire to kill myself for failing at life. Baxter took me in. Gave me a fresh start."

"And made you his errand boy." I stop walking abruptly. "He gave you another direction in which to point that shotgun, instead of at yourself."

Jim snorts and spits on me. "Fuck you, man."

I feel the warmth of his saliva slide down my neck. I reach up to wipe it off.

"Keep moving! I didn't tell you to stop!" he says with a shove. "Just a few more feet to go, cowboy."

The crickets go silent as we continue walking.

"You ever think that you're being used not saved?" I ask.

"Shut up!"

"Maybe Baxter realized that he needed help to run his game. Maybe the game has gotten bigger because his lust for death has grown. More bodies to the slaughterhouse, right? Or slaughter-field—"

"Shut up!"

"And here you come. A suicidal 'loser' like the rest of us, with our problems and our self-justified self-loathing. And he sees an opportunity to have someone to help him out—"

"I said, shut the fuck up!"

"Wake up, Jim. Baxter's using you. He's just a troll who gets profit and pleasure out of luring innocent people to their death. Perverse retribution for being paraplegic." I pause. "Better yet, his disability is just a way to justify the morbid desires that were always there. His

135

physical condition is his excuse—"

"Enough!" Jim strikes me in the back of the head. I'm blinded by pain and stumble forward, collapsing.

Before I have a chance to recover, to stop the stars from revolving around my eyes, Jim hoists me back up to my feet. Feels as if I've just stepped off a moving carousel.

"I lost everything in that recession," Jim tells me, his voice almost a growl. "My job. My house. My wife. My kids." He pushes me forward, keeping me on my death march. "They write country songs about men like me."

When my vision finally recovers, and my head stops spinning, I realize we've reached the forest edge.

"But Baxter showed me that I didn't need any of those things or those people in my life. I only needed to watch out and take care of one person—me."

As the throbbing at the base of my skull subsides, I ask, "And what kind of father does that make you?"

"Oh, Jesus. Spare me. You know as well as I do that kids don't take care of their parents these days. Once they're done with you, they park your ass in a nursing home where you spend the rest of your days playing shuffleboard, pissing in your pants, and glaring into the eyes of other forgotten old farts just like yourself. So fuck my kids." With a shove, he finishes with, "Now get your ass back into the playfield—"

"Wait!"

"What?"

"One last question."

Jim stays quiet for a beat.

"Are you really going to drive Kylie to Miami?" I ask, knowing full well I trust Jim about as far as I can throw him.

Jim responds by sticking me in the lower back with the barrel.

Good.

Now I know exactly where the gun is.

Or at least it's a good estimate.

"Are you really that naive?" he asks with a laugh. "As soon as I get back to the trailer, I'm going to tear into her ass like it's Christmas and then dump her back in the woods when I'm finished."

I feel my blood start to boil.

"Naturally I'll be doing all of this in front of Baxter," Jim says, with the barrel still pressed against my back. "He likes to watch. And I'm not easily embarrassed so I could give two shits."

Now I go blind with rage instead of pain.

All I have to do is spin around and lay into him. I'll have to do it quickly to not get a hole blown in my backside.

"It's a small price to pay for free pussy," Jim says nonchalantly—this is clearly not the first time he's raped a woman and left her to die by the hands of the hunters. "Best part is, there won't be shit you can do about it, cuz you'll either be worm-food or have yourself a nice, new haircut courtesy of them feather heads out there."

It's quickly becoming clear who the real monsters are in this game.

"That answer your question, chief?" Jim asks.

It's now or never.

"It sure does." I whirl around to catch a wide-eyed look of surprise in Jim's eyes as I push aside the shotgun and hammer my fist down onto his nose. A satisfying crack follows. He buckles and stumbles backward, releasing the grip of the shotgun and leaving it in my hands. I twirl it around and take aim.

"This is for all of those you've hurt and killed." I brace the shotgun against my chest. "Especially the women."

"Do it!" Jim grunts through gritted teeth. There's a seething hell-fire in his eyes. The red glow from the forest reflecting the pure evil inside this man. "Pull that trigger. Then you'll become a killer just like me."

"If that means eradicating the world of trash like you, I can live with that." I pull the trigger—

But just as I do, I'm yanked backward.

The blast erupts over Jim's head, missing him completely. My world goes upside down as I'm pulled down to the floor with a painful thud. The shotgun bounces out of my hands, and I'm staring up at a pair of fiery red eyes...

And a scalp-less young man.

Damien.

"I'll take it from here, Jim," he says with a crooked smile.

Before I can react, Damien swings something above his head and brings it down on my face.

And things go dark.

22

The Cookout

My head is yanked upward. I awaken to a bonfire, encircled by a half-dozen hunters. Orange-and-yellow firelight flickers onto their pallid skin. Their eyes ablaze like tiny volcanoes.

Damien emerges from between them, strutting toward me with his mouth slung open, eyes red hot. The dried blood around his head has formed a dark crimson halo that clearly distinguishes where the skin on his head ends, and the bone begins.

I'm pushed down onto my knees. My arms are tied behind my back. Damien grabs my chin and lifts my head so that our faces meet.

"I'm about to give your life new meaning." Damien's breath smells like roadkill. He produces a bone knife. "You'll understand as soon I as stick this in your windpipe."

Well, here it goes. This is how I'm going to die. The truth is, I'm more worried about Kylie than I am about my own life. I need to stall him. Need a moment to figure some way out of this.

"I don't get it," I mumble.

Damien pauses. "What'd you say?"

"I said, I just don't get it."

He cocks his head to the side. "Don't get what?"

"Why you hate me so much. You don't even know me."

Damien trades looks with the other hunters. He explodes with laughter, but they don't share in his outburst. "Cuz I just do. I hate

139

everybody."

"Why?"

Damien takes a deep breath, his nostrils flaring as he says, "Because people suck."

"Why do you say that?" I ask, while really in the back of my mind I'm focusing on how to get out of these restraints.

"What do you mean, why do you say that?" Damien scoffs. "You been under a rock your entire life? People are judgmental assholes." There's rancor in his tone. "I'm tired of people and the way they look at me. Like I'm some kind of fucking freak."

If only Damien had a mirror. He'd see what a monster he's become. He looks like the victim in a murder scene who came back to tell the world about it.

"And what makes you think," I ask, "that people judge you?"

Damien jams his thumb into his chest. "Because I've been me for eighteen years, you dumb-ass!" His eyes flash bright red as he goes on. "I've eaten alone at the lunch table many times, amigo. I was a walking shadow. There were days at school where I never opened my mouth. My grades were shit. Couldn't play sports. I think, given a second chance, my parents would have aborted me." He snarls. "I was the 'oops' baby after all."

While he's busy ranting, I just can't stop thinking about Kylie. I don't want anything to happen to her. But there's not much I can do. These assholes have got me held down tight.

Damien smiles wide, exposing a mouthful of gnarled, crowded teeth. "That wrinkled old weirdo showing up in my dreams was the best thing that could've happened to me."

The shaman.

"Yeah," Damien says as if reading my thoughts. "You know who I'm talking about."

"Never met him."

"Then someone else you know did. And here you are." Damien steps forward and punches me. "All right, enough talking." The blow knocks the wind out of me. I see stars. The kid hits like a heavyweight. To one of the hunters, he makes a slicing motion along his own forehead as he mumbles in the Kenneh'wah tongue. To me, "I told him to scalp ya!"

My captor pulls my head all the way back, so I'm now staring straight up at him. The fire casts an eerie amber haze on his skin. His eyes burn bright with orange hate as he hisses, "Chek-taaaaaah."

Holding me still, he brings his bone knife to my scalp. What will follow will be the slow and steady unzipping of my flesh from my head. Even though this is going to be a horrifically slow death, and the sensation of having my own skin stripped away like a banana peel is going to have me screaming in agony . . .

Still, all I can think about is Kylie.

I have no way of saving her now, and Jim Grimm is going to have his way with her. He's going to use her and leave her here to these maniacs.

And I'll soon be one of them.

"Wait!" I shout.

"Oh, Jesus. What?" Damien asks me, twisting his head to the side. He gestures for the hunter to hold off on the surgery.

"Damien's not your real name, is it?" I ask.

"Of course not." Damien licks his lips. "It was Rupert. Stupid-ass name. But now . . . it's Damien." He claps his hands with psychotic glee and then mumbles in the Kenneh'wah tongue.

I can't help but close my eyes, grit my teeth as I anticipate the pain. The bone knife presses up against my skin, but only for a second. I hear a gurgling noise above me. Then the sound of something falling to the ground. A light thump. All followed by an outburst of protests from the Kenneh'wah.

My eyes open and I'm staring up at my captor, writhing like a fish caught on a hook that it has no hope of escaping from. A bone knife protrudes from his neck.

"YOOOOOOOU!" Damien screeches. "HOW DARE YOU TURN ON

US?"

"Because you killed the wrong man," a deep voice responds as the blade is pulled back out of the hunter. "You killed me."

The dead hunter's body is tossed aside, and I can't believe my eyes.

Can't believe who I'm looking at right now.

"My anger's stronger than your anger," Bear tells Damien.

"We'll see about that." Damien then cries out, "CHEK-TAH!" He chants it several more times as Bear cuts my restraints.

I glance up at Bear, shocked that he's alive—especially with a chunk of flesh missing from the side of his head and gaping wounds all over his body.

The hunters surrounding us all join in on Damien's war cries.

"Bear..." I can hardly speak. "You're . . . you're . . . you're alive?"

Bear pauses for a moment. Then his eyes flash red. Mouth open wide, he lets out a raspy, "Chek-taaaaah."

Oh shit.

So maybe he's not . . . alive.

Maybe he's . . .

One of them after all.

23

Game Changer

The red in Bear's eyes fades, and he pauses momentarily as if snapping out of a daydream. "I don't know how much longer I can hold it back."

"Hold what back?" I ask.

Bear's gaze shifts to Damien and the rest of the Kenneh'wah. "Their rage." His eyes suddenly pulse red once more, and he picks me up by my neck, lifting me at least a foot off the ground. "Our rage!" He shouts with a crooked snarl on his lips and in a voice that's almost inhuman, "Chek-taaaaaaah!"

Bear's grip is fierce. Breathing becomes impossible. A vibrant, sharp pain courses up the sides of my head. An ugly pinching feeling that sends dizzying spots swirling before my eyes.

"That's it, my Kenneh'wah brother," Damien cheers behind me.

The red light in Bear's eyes dims. He whispers to me, "Rodney . . . Damien came here to change the game."

I'm having a tough time processing what that means, considering the oxygen going to my brain is quickly depleting. I mean to ask, "What are you talking about?" but instead a choked gurgle escapes me.

Before Bear can continue, I witness the Kenneh'wah fire-red return to his eyes.

Damien shouts, "Choke the shit outta that punk bitch!"

I bring my hands up to pry Bear's large fingers off my windpipe, but he's got the death grip of an anaconda. So I do the next best thing and kick him square in the nuts. He howls and drops me. The fiery red in his eyes dwindles.

And for a moment, the world seems to pause.

And Bear's eyes lock with mine.

And he says, "Move."

Before I can respond, he pushes me aside and hurls his bone knife right at Damien. It hits him in the chest, sending him screaming and stumbling backward.

Damien tries to pull out the blade, but it has lodged itself in his rib cage. "HOW DARE YOU TURN ON US AGAIN?!"

The other Kenneh'wah move in to attack, but Bear goes on a rampage. He grabs the closest hunter, lifts him up in the air like a trophy, and tosses him into the bonfire—where he promptly lights up like a dead Christmas tree. Amazingly the hunter jumps back to his feet, only to stumble around the campsite uselessly, arms flailing and still very much engulfed in flames. He collapses on the ground, a heap of burning dead flesh.

The war cries come from every direction now.

There's a frenzy of battle in the air.

Two hunters flank Bear from either side, but before they can both close in on him, he clotheslines one of them and knocks them on their ass. Bear spins around, elbows the second hunter, splits his nose in half, then drives him to the ground.

Bear straddles the fallen hunter, cracks his neck, and steals his knife. He rises and turns just in time to stuff the blade into the stomach of the other hunter—there's a moment of surprise in that hunter's face, but that's quickly interrupted as Bear hikes the blade up into the hunter's midsection, burying the blade right down to its hilt.

Three more hunters surround Bear before he can get the jump on them. They pile in and suffocate him in a twisted mangle of arms, hands, and teeth. I hear him scream out as they stab, bite, and tear at his flesh. His eyes oscillating between various shades of red.

As Bear struggles to free himself from the hunters, Damien approaches. "Guess I have to kill you again, fatboy." He grabs Bear by what's left of his hair and pulls his head back. A sneer forms across his face. "So much for second chances." Damien manages to yank the knife out of his own chest and holds the blade right in front of Bear's eyes.

Bear lets out, "RODNEY! RUNNNNNNNNNN!"

Damien snaps his head in my direction, aims the knife at me, and shouts, "Don't let that cocksucker get away!"

Too late.

I've already taken off.

Behind me I hear the footfalls of one, two, three—God, who knows how many—Kenneh'wah close behind me.

Beyond that, I hear Bear's hoarse screams of agony. That man has saved my life twice in one night. I need to make it out of this alive, not just for Kylie's sake, but to let Bear's daughters know that their father died a hero.

But then again . . .

Yeah . . .

First I have to make it out of here alive.

24

You're Next

Now I'm just running.

No idea which way is east or west. I just know I got to keep going. Got to escape these maniacs and find Baxter's base camp so I can spare Kylie from getting raped, murdered, or whatever else they have planned. However, the faster I run, the more my legs burn. The more my side starts to cramp. All this anxiety and exertion without a moment to rest or to eat is taking a toll on both mind and body. Fatigue alone is one thing. Fighting and fatigue are worse.

I trip over a tree stump and face-plant into a thick patch of moss, taking in a mouthful of the vegetation. Tastes like crap. Lucky I fell where I did. A few inches farther and I would've crowned myself with a rock the size of a bowling ball.

"Chek-taaaaaaah!"

I flip onto my back in time to see a hunter beelining straight for me, spear raised in the air.

Oh crap!

He flings the spear, and I roll over just as it catches my shirt, nailing me to the ground. As I try to wriggle the spear free, a knee collides with my gut, and the hunter straddles me. Spouting Kenneh'wah gibberish, he pulls out a tomahawk.

If I only I had a weapon, a knife, something I could fight back with. I'd gladly take Chase's butter knife if that were my only option. Better than being empty-handed.

"CHEK-TAH!" the hunter says with a hiss.

He raises the tomahawk to strike, but before he can hit me with it, I reach up above my head, catch ahold of that rock that had nearly crowned me, and with one swift motion, jam it up into the base of his chin. There's a satisfying crunch, followed by him toppling over, dazed and in pain. He lands next to me, writhing, trying to recover.

I give up on the idea of removing the spear. Not enough leverage to make that happen, so instead, I tear my shirt in half. As I get to my feet, the red in the hunter's eyes intensifies. Before he gets a chance to stand, I pull the spear out of the ground with little effort now and bring it down on the hunter, pinning him down just as he tried to do to me. The spear goes clean through his torso. I lean all my body weight on it, making sure it's in him all the way. Bubbles of spit and blood erupt from his mouth as he mumbles incoherently to me.

"That's for Bear," I tell the hunter while still catching my breath. The splash of light in his neon eyes fades, and I can't help but gawk at him, half in contempt, half in confusion.

Why have these monsters come back from their graves?

Then again, as Mac said, they were never buried—

The horrid sounds of war cries and a half dozen footfalls close in. Before I can make a move, two more hunters appear. They rush straight for me. One of them chucks a spear at me, and I nearly trip trying to dodge it. It lands just inches from my feet. I pick it up and throw it right back at him—and thankfully he's so close that I don't miss. The spear hits him in the gut. He screams and falls to the ground, disappearing into a thicket of wild bushes.

The other hunter wails, a ball of hatred unraveling from within the depths of his chest. With head tucked low, arms raised, two bone knives in his hands, he charges at me as if he's a tortured bull finally freed from its pen.

Free to run down his captors.

As he closes in, I notice just how huge this hunter is. This bull of a

Kenneh'wah warrior looks as though he throws around logs for sport.

I scoop up the other hunter's fallen tomahawk and run at the bull. Just as we're about to collide, I swing the tomahawk and catch his jaw. There's a satisfying thwap sound as stone connects with bone. The bull's head spins—but snaps back to face me just as quickly.

For a moment, I detect an expression on his face that asks, Is that all you've got? Followed by him kicking me with such insane force that I go flying backward, slam into a tree and slump to the ground. Feels like I took a battering ram to the chest. I push through the pain, get to my feet . . .

The bull is already on me. He brings down both knives, but I drop into a squat, and the knives plunge into the thick bark of the tree. He tries to pull them out, but not before I snatch up the tomahawk once more and swing it up between his legs.

The bull lets out a roar. He cups his groin with one hand, and sucker punches me in the face with the other. The blow sends me reeling, stumbling off to one side. I tumble to the ground, and the tomahawk flies out of my grip. Before I can even catch my breath, the bull picks me up by my throat and tosses me a good five feet. The cold, hard earth meets my body with a dull crack. The back of my head bounces against the ground, sending a tremor through my skull that rattles my brain.

I'm staring up at the night sky, a canopy of stars, twinkling down their sparkling white light from millions of miles away. Their brightness begins to fade as I start to pass out . . .

Come on, Rodney!

Don't stop now.

Kylie's depending on you.

There's the sound of heavy footsteps, then wood snapping. I blink several times to find the bull standing over me, one leg on either side of mine, bone knives in both hands once more.

"Ket'ya nek tat ono," he says a deep, baritone voice. He points at me. "Tat yak kule jat'nyo, chek-tah."

"I have no idea"—I can barely get the words out—"what the hell you're saying, asshole."

"He said . . ." I hear the voice of an old man, and Mac emerges from behind the bull, shotgun in hand. "Even an invader like you can be molded into a warrior. Damien is our new chief. He will lead us to our retribution." His eyes pulse red as he says, "Don't worry. Once our spirit is inside you, you'll understand."

"I already understand." With every ounce of energy left in my body, I bring my leg up and drive my heel square into the bull's knee, shattering his kneecap as though it were made of glass. Howling in pain, he drops his knives, buckles over, and clutches his knee with both hands.

I roll to one side and hop onto my feet—just as the dirt explodes next to me.

A ghostly plume of smoke rises from the tip of Mac's gun barrel.

My eyes open wide as he pulls the trigger and I flinch—

Click.

A look of surprise on Mac's face. He fumbles to reload, but not before I nab one of the bull's knives from the ground and charge the old man, knocking him clear off his feet. We both go down, me on top, the shotgun laid flat between us. Mac pushes the gun against me as if he were trying to bench-press me off him. He's certainly vigorous for his age, but then again, he's not 100 percent himself.

He's not human anymore.

He's something else.

But with all my body weight pressing back down against him, he struggles to get me off him. Through gritted teeth, spittle forming around his mouth, Mac says, "You won't . . . survive . . . the night. No one's ever survived."

I lean over the shotgun, wrap one around arm it, freeing up my other hand, which is still holding the blade—and I shove the knife straight through the semi-circle of soft flesh under Mac's chin.

"There's a first time," I say as I bury the knife in his head, "for everything!"

The light in Mac's eyes fades until they glow no more.

Behind me, I hear the bull mumbling in his native tongue.

I grab the shotgun and roll onto my back. The bull comes staggering toward me, dragging his injured leg, eyes burning as if powered by the sun. Instinctively I pull the trigger—

Click!

Oh yeah . . . it's out of shells.

Remembering I pocketed a few shells of my own, I fish one out and with trembling hands, pop one in the chamber—

Bull cracks me across the face with a clenched fist. Before I can even blink, a follow-up punch to the face sends my head spinning in the other direction. Still, somehow, I manage not to lose my grip on the shotgun—

Bull pushes me by my shoulders, pins me to the ground. Bastard weighs about a thousand pounds.

"Kannu pah no lek na, Chek-tah!" He punches me again, and I am rewarded with the taste of blood in my mouth and the jarring of my vision. There's no way I can bring up the shotgun to use it. One of my hands is trapped at my side, the other is locked against the trigger guard. If I were to shoot now, I'd blow off my own shoulder.

"Oyo kannu, Chek-tah!"

Whatever he's saying, I'm sure it isn't good, because he's managed to yank the bone knife from Mac's skull and is about to put it into mine, when I do the only thing I can—

I grab his broken kneecap with the hand that's pinned to my waist and squeeze. I squeeze it like a rotten grapefruit, jamming my thumb in-between cartilage and bone or whatever the hell he's made of. Bull freaks, screeches his lungs out. For a split second, I fear that he'll jam the knife into me out of sheer reflex, but instead he leans back, turns his head toward his knee, and grabs my hand, squeezing it equally hard. I yell out in pain, too, but the diversion is just enough for me to bring the shotgun up with my other hand and pull the trigger.

Bull's chest explodes. I'm sprayed with flesh, blood, and bone.

Hands quivering, eyes fading to black, the bull slides off me. I take a moment to catch my breath. My hands are trembling. My body hurts in a hundred places. I feel parts of my face swelling up from the blows.

No time to rest.

Got to keep going.

War cries echo in the distance. Damien won't be too far behind.

I get to my feet, grab one of the bone knives and reload my shotgun. Only a few shells left. Going to make them count.

A quick glance in all directions, and I realize I'm completely lost. Which way is which?

As if the universe, God, or Baxter were answering my question, a flare goes off in the distance. I'm not too far away from it.

Is that east? Must be. But does it matter now? If I stay where I'm at, I'll have to deal with Damien (aka Rupert) and his mob.

Wait . . .

This is just too coincidental.

Why did that flare go off just now...?

Something tells me to look up, and I do. Above me are several cameras staring me down, each one aglow with a faint red LED light. Of course! Baxter mentioned these earlier. He's been influencing our every move. An invisible hand guiding us. Rats in a maze toward our fate . . .

Whatever fate he decides.

Baxter doesn't want me to give up. He wants me to keep playing. The longer I play, the longer I survive. The longer I survive, the more exciting things get—the bigger his hard-on.

The more people continue to watch.

I look up at the cameras, chest heaving. A mixture of exhaustion and exasperation with each breath. I gaze right into the beady little red LED light of the cameras as if I could look through them to see a very corpulent, disgusting, withering old man staring back at me from the comfort and safety of his trailer.

He or Jim better not have laid a single finger on Kylie.

If I make it there . . .

Correction.

When I make it there, those two men will see a side of me no one has ever seen.

A side of me I know I've never seen myself.

Time to send Baxter a message. I move into an opening in the trees where the full moon shines down a beam of white light on me. I stand so that Baxter can see me clearly.

I give him the finger and clearly mouth the words:

YOU'RE NEXT.

25

Mad Dash

Maybe this is what Baxter wants. Perhaps he's had his own death wish all along, but he's too much of a pussy to kill himself by his own hands. Maybe this is what it's all about—seeing who is tough enough to survive his game, hunt him down for a change, and put him into the ground.

Or maybe I'm completely wrong.

Maybe he just wants to keep the game going for as long as I can survive. The longer the game goes, the more interesting it gets for him. Either way, his warped motivations don't matter. The only thing I care about now is rescuing Kylie and escaping.

I race through the trees. Branches are whipping me in the face here and there. My legs are worn out. If I never have to run again, it'll be too soon.

One of the hunters jumps in my path.

"CHEK-TAH!"

I charge him and crack the butt of the shotgun several times across his skull. He doesn't even get a chance to react. He wails, and he drops to the ground. I keep moving, not bothering to look back. If any of these other hunters get in my way now, I'll take them down all the same. Nothing is going to stop me.

Not even Damien.

I'm hoping that little prick shows up so I can feed him a mouthful of buckshot. But he doesn't, and before I know it, I'm back at the clearing, back at the campsite outlined by the hazy glow of the spotlights encircling it. Up ahead sit Baxter's two RVs along with a newer model Ford truck. Someone stands next to it.

Jim . . . peering into the scope of his shotgun—

A chunk of grass bursts at my feet. I jump back. There's a distant click. Bark explodes behind me. I drop low to the ground.

Jim steadies his shotgun on the truck's hood. Reloads.

I make a mad dash back into the woods as another bullet hits the ground where I was a second ago.

That stupid flare . . .

It was just another trap.

Jim used it to get me out in the open so that he could pick me off. But why? Because I've become a viable opponent? Surprisingly adept at killing off Baxter's beloved hunters?

"Goddammit!" Jim smacks the hood. Cocks the shotgun. Aims.

In the depths of the forest, I hear the hunters making their way in my direction. The sound of Jim's gun is most likely drawing their attention.

I've got a choice to make. If I make a run for the RVs, I'll have to clear the field before Jim can pick me off; get close enough to him to hit him with my shotgun.

If I stay here the tribe is going to find me. One against how many hunters?

There's a loud pop above my head. Tree bark showers me.

Jim's aim is getting better. "Come on out, you little shit!" he shouts.

I hear movement. I glance over my shoulder. The silhouettes of hunters leaping over shrubs and fallen logs draw ever so closer. They're headed straight for me. I turn back to Jim who's patiently waiting, monitoring my position with his shotgun. Can't stay here much longer. However, the minute I step foot onto the clearing there's a chance Jim will nail me.

The war cries get louder. Another glance back toward the forest.

The hunters are maybe all of thirty feet away, spears and tomahawks in hand.

"RODNEEEEEY!"

Damien.

Great. Now that little shithead shows up.

"OHHH RODNEEEY!" Damien sings my name. "RODNEY, BOYYYYYYYYYY!"

"Come on out, ya chicken-shit!" Jim yells from across the clearing. His eye never leaves his shotgun's scope. "Come face me!"

Either I take my chances with Damien's hunting party or attempt a fifty-yard dash before Jim puts a hole in me.

"RODNEY!" I don't dare look back, but I can tell Damien is right behind me when he cries, "WE SEEEEEEEEEE YOU!"

Screw it.

I leap out into the clearing just as I feel the air whoosh behind my neck. Some hunter took a swipe at me and missed.

"GOTCHA!" Jim shouts with glee, but before he can fire a shot, a white stream of light—a flare—sails right into him. Nails him in the torso. His gun goes off, and he misses me as he drops to the ground, trying desperately to rip his shirt off to avoid catching on fire.

And while he's busy screaming and rolling around, I bolt across the field and run right up to him. He's managed to tear the now burning shirt off his body, and looks up at me as though surprised to find me standing above him, shotgun pointed right at his ugly face—a face that's adorned with a shiny, black eye.

"Where is she?" I ask Jim.

"What? I don't know!"

"Did you touch her?"

He shakes his head vigorously.

"Don't lie to me!"

"I swear! I didn't touch her, cowboy." Jim starts to raise his hand.

"EASY!"

"Actually..." He holds up both hands in surrender, points at the black-and-blue shiner surrounding his eyeball. "That funky-haired bitch sucker punched me before I could lay a finger on her. Then she stole my flare gun and ran off!"

Kylie is still alive.

She's out there.

"Get up!" I gesture for Jim to get to his feet. "Let's get your boss out here so we can wrap this up."

Jim rises.

"Keep your hands up!" I tell him. My trigger finger is itching to send this asshole into next week.

Jim puts one hand up, reaches slowly toward his waist.

"Hey!" I bark. "I said hands up!"

"If you want Baxter"—around Jim's waist is a small walkie-talkie—"I have to radio him, genius—"

"No need!" a voice calls out behind Jim. Baxter is already on his porch. Gun in one hand, shot glass in the other. "This is my world, son. I know everything that's going on." He takes a swig. "So . . . what would you like to wrap up?"

26

The Dream Connection

"I want to wrap up this game," I tell Baxter.

"OK. Fine. But first, we'll start with you lowering your gun," Baxter says with a nod as several guns cock behind me.

I lower the shotgun.

"Lay it on the ground." Baxter points downward.

I hesitate and then feel the cold steel of a gun barrel press against my neck.

Reluctantly I do as told.

"I've really enjoyed watching you fight for your life," Baxter says. "You're very much like Jim."

"I'm nothing like this asshole," I say.

"Yeah, I'll second that," Jim says with a scoff.

"No-no-no-no." Baxter waves a finger in the air. "You've got a renewed fervor for life. It's evident in your actions and your character."

Fury and frustration swell inside me as I stare Baxter down. If only I could shoot him with my eyeballs.

"So rather than continue the game," Baxter says with a bit of a smirk. "How about you come work for me? You have more than surpassed my expectations." With a chuckle, he then says, "Jim could use the help."

Jim sneers. "I could?"

Can't believe I'm hearing this.

Baxter tells Jim, "The game always needs more players." He looks at me. "And you could help him recruit and direct more people our way. Not to mention, we could use another handyman now that Mac is gone."

"Try Craigslist," I say.

"I don't need to beg for applicants when they come to me. And I really could use a second set of hands." Baxter points at the other trailer. "You see that RV there. It houses computers, monitors, servers, routers. All that necessary IT shit to keep the streaming uninterrupted. To keep my movie going." He laughs to himself as he pulls a flask from his side pocket. "You should see my electric bill. Takes a lot of AC to keep that trailer from becoming one big oven."

"I'm sure you can afford it," I say.

"Funny you say that. In addition to all the back of the house hardware, that trailer's also where I keep my safe. It's loaded to the gills with all the cash and jewelry of those who couldn't survive the night. Ironic, isn't it? The hunted fund the death of future victims." He takes a sip. "You'd be privy to a portion of those earnings. There's more there than you'd think."

"I'd rather take a bullet to the head than work for you."

"We both know how that played out for you the last time," Baxter says with a chuckle. "Let me ask you something."

I try to turn to get a glimpse of the number of thugs standing behind me—but a nudge to my backside stops me short.

"You think it was a coincidence that your sister called you right when you were about to blow out the back of your skull?"

"Let me guess . . . your supposed shaman led the way," I say. "I already heard the story."

Baxter waves a stubby finger in the air again. "No, you've only heard part of the story." He takes another sip, wipes his lips with his sleeve, and angles the flask in my direction. "Care for a swig?"

I glare at him, wanting nothing more than the opportunity to bash his face in.

"You might need it after you hear what I'm about to tell you," he says, smiling from ear to ear like the glib little monster he is.

I say nothing.

Baxter shrugs with a suit-yourself gesture. "Since you were looking to blow your brains out, the shaman picked up on your suicidal intent. But unlike some folks who've seen the shaman in dreams and visions, you weren't as easily guided here by his telepathic influence."

"Telepathic influence? Give me a break. They're just dreams," I say. "The fact that this old man appeared in people's heads was a coincidence."

"Coincidence? OK, Carl Jung." Baxter snickers. "You know even he believed in telepathy. He understood that telepathy was not something to be coined as supernatural, per se, but something that we could not presently comprehend. He also understood that not everyone was susceptible to telepathic influence."

"What are you getting at?" I ask.

"Mac may have been nuts, but he wasn't wrong." He leans forward, eyes narrowing. "Your sister, Becky, was the one who inadvertently led you here."

I shake my head. "What are you talking about?"

"All the shaman did was sense your desire to end your life. Homed in on it like a psychic missile. It was your sister that did the rest of the heavy lifting. You two must have some serious connection that you are both unaware of. Maybe you dreamed of her because you missed her. Or whatever." Baxter grins, and it almost appears forced. "And with one little dream, the shaman linked the two of you together. Then he influenced her dreams."

I'm finding all this hard to process.

Understatement.

I'm finding this entire night hard to process.

"Isn't that ironic?" Baxter takes another swig. Sighs as if pleased with himself. "The very person who saved you from killing yourself unknowingly led you right into death's playground."

Anger surges inside me once more.

"Anyway . . . we're done shooting the shit." Baxter nods toward the horizon.

A fresh wash of sunlight reaches up toward the clouds.

"Morning's coming. I've got future games to set up and could use your help," he says. "So, are you in or out?"

"I'm out."

"All right, then," with a dismissive wave of the hand, Baxter tells Jim, "Kill him."

"'Bout fucking time!" Jim snatches up the shotgun. "I was falling asleep." Then to me, he says, "Close your eyes or keep 'em open. I don't care." He checks the gun to see that it's still loaded. "Adios, muchacho!"

I close my eyes, expecting my face to explode at any moment from the unyielding blast of buckshot.

But then all hell breaks loose.

27

The Square Dance

There's a scream behind me followed by a light so bright I can see it even with my eyes closed. I open my eyes to find one of Baxter's men screaming. White sparks jumping from his chest. He's been shot with a flare . . .

I'm pushed from behind and knocked to the ground.

"Stay down," one of the men says.

The screams continue. Then, "Someone, please help me!"

"Carter!" Jim responds. "Dammit, Carter. Just roll on the ground!"

"I am!" Carter screams as he does as he's told.

Then someone else asks, "Where the hell did that flare come from?"

"From that bitch!" Jim yells as he looks over his shoulder.

Beyond him, Baxter shouts and points furiously toward the trees. He's so upset, he nearly lifts himself out of his wheelchair. "She can't escape!"

In the direction of Baxter's anger, a lone shadow stands still, watching us. Can't tell if it's Kylie or someone else.

"Hurry, before she gets away!" Baxter yells.

"But the Kenneh'wah?" one of the men protests.

"It's nearly dawn," Jim says. "They'll be asleep soon if they haven't crashed already."

The mysterious shadow disappears into the woods. The sun peeks up over the horizon. Several golden rays light up the undersides of the clouds.

I've never been so happy to see a sunrise in my life.

"That includes you too, Carter," Jim says.

"Dude, I'm burned pretty bad." There's a circle of puffy pink and black flesh on Carter's chest. Looks like a giant cigarette burn. He touches it and winces. "Fucking hurts, man. I think I need a doctor."

"You'll survive."

"What are you people waiting for?" Baxter cries.

Jim keeps the gun on me but looks to the men as he shouts, "You heard him. Get going!"

The men head toward the forest. There's a hesitation in their steps that suggests they're a little reluctant to go into the woods.

Jim adds, "And don't you pussies come back without her."

And that's when I charge Jim, trapping the shotgun against his chest. His head spins to face me, nostrils flaring, brow furrowed, a look of surprise and anger. I grab the brim of his newsboy cap and yank it over his eyes and then hammer him in the nose with my fist. He lets out a grunt, loosens his grip, and I tear away the shotgun.

I take a step back and bring up the gun to shoot, but Jim's lanky arm swats the barrel to the side as I pull the trigger. The wake of the blast misses him completely. Before I can squeeze off another round, he drives his fist into my stomach. Every bit of air is forced out of my body at once. I buckle over, a right hook glances the left side of my face, sending me sideways—but Jim catches me. He yanks the shotgun from my hand and pushes me back.

"Who do you think you're messing with, chief?" Jim asks.

I sway, woozy from the blows. Blood seeps into my mouth. That last punch sliced open my lip. I'm struggling to catch my breath. Feels like he knocked more than the wind out of me. Feels like he almost beat the life out of me. I hoist myself up, knees wobbly, head spinning and straighten my back. "You're a dead man," I tell him.

"A dead man? You mean me?" Jim asks raising an eyebrow. "'Fraid you got that all wrong, amigo."

"I'm not"—I lick the blood off my lip—"your friend."

"You're right." Jim braces the shotgun against his chest. "I don't have any friends." He's about to squeeze the trigger when Baxter calls out his name.

"Dammit, we need him alive!" Baxter shouts.

"We do?" Jim asks.

"For right this moment, yes. We do." Baxter wheels off the trailer porch toward us.

"Why? Why don't we just kill him?" Jim pauses. The wheels turning in his head. "I mean, you were more than happy for me to shoot him a moment ago."

"Because now it's obvious we have something that woman wants," Baxter says as he joins us.

"You mean lover boy here?"

"Yes, Jim. Him!" Baxter points at me. "She's protecting him. That means she wants him alive." Baxter pulls out a walkie-talkie from his wheelchair bag. Speaking slowly and deliberately, he says, "Boys, you copy?"

At first static, then a muffled, "Go ahead."

"If you see the girl, let her know that we have Rodney, and if she doesn't surrender, I'm going to cut off his head and balls and mail them to her home." Baxter pauses, then asks, "Copy?"

The walkie crackles. "Copy."

Baxter lowers the walkie, then turns to Jim. "If we go down, I'll make sure she lives to regret it. That she'll know it's her fault this man dies. Make sense?"

"I guess," Jim says with a shrug, shotgun still aimed at me. This time his gaze never breaks from mine.

It's getting brighter by the minute. If what these assholes are saying is true, at least Kylie won't have the Kenneh'wah hunting her down. However, she'll still have three of Baxter's goons to deal with.

Baxter then says, "Now bring Rodney into my trailer and tie him up."

Jim lets out a defiant chuckle. "Are you serious?"

Baxter smacks the arm of his wheelchair. "Yes, goddammit, I'm serious!"

"Let's just kill him. He's a wild card we don't need. Besides"—Jim nods his chin toward the woods—"that stupid bitch ain't going anywhere. We're miles away from civilization."

"I know exactly where we're at because this land belongs to me!" Baxter's gaze darkens. "And let's not also forget that you work for me. Now do what I said!"

Jim hesitates. "Last I checked"—his eyes narrow—"I'm the one holding the gun."

"Oh." There's a hint of amusement in Baxter's tone. "Is that a threat?"

"Maybe."

"That's what I thought." Baxter puts a finger to his lips as if deep in thought, then continues. "Well, if you kill me, then I guess there'll be no one to stop one of my employees from releasing the footage of you shooting me, as well as the footage of the others you've murdered outside the playing field." He giggles as he interlaces his fingers. "Oh . . . and all of the women you've raped."

Even through his thick beard, I can tell Jim is biting his lip. Holding back. Unsure if what he's hearing is true.

"What?" Baxter asks as he unfolds his fingers and shrugs. "Did you really think that I trusted you? Or anyone here for that matter? If my employee in Miami doesn't hear from me every morning, he knows that something has gone terribly wrong, and after he reviews the video and sees that it was you who killed me, he'll get you your fifteen minutes of fame across the fucking Internet."

"Bullshit."

"Shoot me and find out."

Jim takes a deep breath. He's grasping the shotgun so tightly his knuckles have gone white.

"Or do what I say, and bring Romeo here inside."

"I'll meet you halfway." He pumps the shotgun several times, ejecting the unspent rounds into the night. He then tosses the gun aside.

"What are you doing?" Baxter asks, wide-eyed.

"I'll bring him inside all right." Jim raises his fists to shield his face. "After I'm done with him."

"Fine. Have fun." Baxter waves dismissively and wheels himself back toward the RV. His voice trails off as he says, "You'd just better not lose."

"I won't. Now go pour yourself a drink and take a nap. Let me handle the dirty work... just like I always do."

"You like it," Baxter says as he retires inside the trailer.

"Yes, I do." To me, Jim then says, "Now . . . as for you . . ." His shoulders rise and fall like pistons as he squares off with me. "Show me what you got."

I wipe the blood from my lip and bring my hands up, too. Jim circles me like a clock arm. I keep time with him, spinning in the center of our fight circle, waiting for him to enter and strike.

"Come on, chief!" He gestures for me to take a swing. "Bring it."

I don't. Instead, I keep my hands up, square up my hips, bending slightly at the knees, grounding myself. My palms are open in anticipation for any blow that might come my way; unlike Jim, who's got his fists clenched, which wastes energy. That's something that my friend Phil had mentioned to me on that bus ride back from aikido camp. Every taut muscle uses up precious energy that leads to fatigue.

Knowing this is one thing.

Practicing this while the adrenaline's pumping and my limbs are quivering is another.

Jim steps sideways, circling me. "I said come on, motherfucker!" Half of his face is hidden behind his lanky forearms. "Come at me. I can see it in your eyes. You wanna take me down? What are you waiting for?"

Adrenaline and fear course through my veins. Sure, I've had years of martial-arts training, but that doesn't make me devoid of nerves and intimidation. It doesn't make me some kind of superhuman warrior. Black belts don't dodge bullets any better than anyone else.

That's the stuff of movies.

"You're more afraid of me than those feather heads, aren't ya?" Jim asks, with a hint of glee in his tone. "Aren't ya! Well, you oughta be."

Jim is bigger than me. He's got reach. He's got stamina. And he's not wiped out from an endless night of running, hiding, and fighting.

My heart is knocking against my chest. I'm trying to steady my breath.

Jim roars and then charges in, fists striking me like a hailstorm of stones. He lands a punch to my lower ribs. Then my cheekbone. Then my stomach. I stagger, try to counter, to block the blows, but it all just comes out as one fumbled mess. The punches keep coming, an incessant beating from all directions. All my time spent on the canvas mat, or testing for my black belt at aikido camp, seems to have evaporated from my memory. This is no doubt the result of fatigue, fear, and nerves. I've spent all my energy fighting off the hunters, and now my body and mind have gone to mush.

"That all you got?" Jim yells as he continues relentlessly pummeling me.

I'm amazed I'm still standing. Maybe it's the sheer force of his opposing blows that are steadying me in place like some human punching bag. A solid right hook cracks me across the jaw.

That drops me.

Jim straddles me. Locks his hands around my throat. Things go south quick.

"No one survives this game but me." Buried in the wispy black-and-gray hairs of Jim's beard is a sneer. "You hear me?"

A nasty throbbing ache spreads across my head.

"Baxter's an idiot. We don't need you as bait." There's bloodlust in Jim's deep, beady eyes. "Because that funky-haired bitch isn't going to get very far." Through clenched teeth, Jim manages a chuckle.

"Trust me. Been at this a long time."

Every vein in my neck is struggling to do its job.

"Even if our men don't find her, she'll circle back looking for your sorry ass." Drops of sweat fall from Jim's forehead and land in my eyes, stinging like acid—but that's the least of my problems. Beyond a wheeze, I can barely get any air into my lungs.

"I'm going to leave your dead body right here." Jim's hands are like vice-grips crushing my windpipe. "And when she comes running for you . . ."

My arms flail uselessly to swat at him. He shrugs them off with little effort.

"I'll jump her. And I'll choke her."

My head feels as though it wants to explode. I'm gasping for any ounce of air I can get. I'm trying to rally what little strength I have.

But it's not enough.

A spray of spittle showers my face as Jim says, "All while humping her right next to your corpse." Jim's snarl curls up into a smile. "Romantic, right?"

In one last attempt, I bring both arms up and reach for his neck, but I'm too weak; too starved for air to do anything. Jim laughs in response.

My vision fades . . .

But something weird happens.

There's a wave of red light that blasts across the field. At first, my dying brain thinks that this is what happens before you go. But then I notice that Jim sees it, too. He releases his grip, and I gasp as if emerging from the ocean itself.

"What the fuck?" Jim mouths as the red glow highlights the underside of his face. The entire RV park lights up.

"HE'S MINE!" a very angst-ridden, raspy voice calls out.

Jim leans back, still straddling me and cranes his neck, trying to get a visual of who's talking. I turn my head to the side, struggling to get as much air back into my lungs as possible. My skull is pounding.

The sound of several footsteps grows louder. Jim narrows his eyes to get a better view, then his expression changes to shock. "Who the hell are you?"

The footsteps are closer now.

Definitely sounds like more than one person.

"I'm Damien."

Jim scoops up the shotgun. "Nice to meet you, Damien." He aims the shotgun.

Click.

"Shit." The word comes out almost a whisper as Jim suddenly remembers that he ejected the rounds just moments earlier.

There's a whooshing sound.

Several arrows pierce Jim's chest.

And one arrow lands square in his eye.

28

Party's Over

Surprisingly Jim is still alive. He's one resilient prick. A thick river of blood rains down from his eye socket and onto his beard. Slowly, he glances down at me, the shaft of the arrow protruding from his skull. He opens his mouth to speak, but only blood comes out.

Another arrow lands in Jim's throat. He lets out a muffled groan, twitches erratically, and falls off me.

Behind me, I hear someone approaching. I rise, turn, and freeze in place. The end of the tip of a spear is hovering inches from my eyeballs. The hunter holding it cocks his head to the side and bears his fangs. These things are even creepier in daylight with their waxy, shimmering, dolphin-gray skin. Eyes and teeth gleaming. The blood on their bodies, dried and reddish-brown.

Damien cuts between the hunters, leans close to Jim's face. Speaks to him as if the man is somehow still alive. Though I doubt it. "I wasn't crying, you piece of shit." Damien wipes at his eyes. "My mascara was running because that bus was a fucking sauna!" He straightens up. Looks at me. "Morning, sunshine. Miss me?"

"No," I say as I survey the RV park. The red glow is everywhere, covering the ground as far as the eye can see. Whatever protection spell was here is gone now. And as far as the Kenneh'wah and their nap time? Seems that's changed as well. But how?

I turn back to Damien, "I didn't miss you, Rupert."

Damien slaps me. "MY NAME IS DAMIEN!" Feels as though I've been smacked by a two-by-four. The kid has hands made of wood. "Get it right!"

I taste the tang of blood in my mouth as the gash on my lip leaks like a sieve. I open and close my jaw several times and feel it click at the joint. If I escape tonight with only TMJ and a busted lip, it'll be a miracle.

I scan the tree line for movement but don't see any sign of Kylie. With several of Baxter's men and countless hunters still out on the prowl, her odds of surviving are worsening by the minute.

"Hey!" Damien snaps his finger several times. "Eyes up here, homie. Let's finish what we started."

I look up at Damien. The pearlescent exposed surface of his skull gleams slick with dark blood under the morning sun. He is a disgusting mess of gore. A Halloween version of his former self. My gaze trails down to his neck. He's wearing a necklace that I don't recall seeing before.

Damien catches me looking at it and smiles. "You like it?" He hooks it with his thumb, lifts it slightly off his chest. There are over a dozen thin, yellow stones fed through a coarse string—but as I look closer, I see those are not stones . . .

They're teeth.

"It's a Kenneh'wah tradition that when their chieftain dies, one of their teeth is pulled and added to this very necklace." Damien jangles it, and the teeth clink together. "Centuries of unsettled vengeance all strung together. Mac gave it to me when he joined us. Right before you killed him!" A glint of red flashes in his eyes. "He stole it from Baxter one night while the fat-ass was stone drunk and Jimmy-boy was busy with the ladies."

The hunters surround me.

A pair of hands push down on my shoulders, and I'm forced to my knees.

Damien continues, "The Kenneh'wah were waiting for someone like

170

me. Someone with balls and a score to settle." He taps the necklace. "This is the gasoline. And I am the dynamite."

"All hail King Damien," I say under my breath.

Damien juts out his chin as he says through clenched teeth, "Pretty much."

One of the hunters grabs my hair and yanks my head back. Damien licks his lips as he brings the knife up to my scalp. "I want to look in your eyes," he says, "as I peel back your scalp. I want you to know pain."

And there's a shit-eating grin on his face that shows that he's OK with that.

More so, he's embraced it.

"If you're lucky," he says, "I might let you come back as one of us."

"Please don't," I say.

Damien snarls. "I'll make that decision!"

There's a gurgled grunt. Jim's body twitches. He's turning. Coming back to life. Becoming one of them.

But Damien seizes a tomahawk from one of the hunters. Pounds Jim's head into the ground until it's mush. Between Baxter, Jim, and Damien, I'm not sure who's the sickest of the three.

Damien tosses the tomahawk aside. Shrugs. "Jim wasn't invited back." He pulls out a bone knife. "Now, where were we?"

I try to stall him by asking, "I thought this RV park was protected?"

"Um, no." Damien pauses. "No more protection spells. Mac came to us. Taught me the shaman's chant. And how to unbind it. Besides," he says, pointing the knife toward the park, "this is all our land anyway. None of it should be protected from us."

"You're not Kenneh'wah," I tell him. "You're a punk kid from the suburbs."

Something wicked explodes in Damien's eyes. "Their blood is in my veins now." He knocks the hunter's hand off my head and grabs my hair, pulling it painfully upward. He presses the blade against my forehead. "I'm going to enjoy this."

"No'h kala no'h koloh!" a voice bellows.

Damien freezes. Looks up. Narrows his eyes. He releases me and steps back. He points the blade toward the voice and barks in Kenneh'wah to several of the hunters. They take off running. I turn to see where they're headed.

Baxter is on the porch of his RV. Shotgun in hand. The quartet of hunters stampede toward him. He fires, and one of the hunters squeals and drops dead. But the others are fast approaching.

The shotgun roars again.

Another hunter drops.

Baxter aims and pulls the trigger, but he's out of rounds.

"No'h kala no'h koloh!" Baxter tries rolling himself back inside the RV, but in his wheel snags on something and he's dumped onto the ground. He moans in pain, flips himself over onto his stomach, and just as the hunters surround him, he smacks the ground as he cries out once more, "No'h kala no'h koloh!"

The hunters suddenly stop in their tracks.

The red glow on the ground around Baxter dims. The eerie light fades away in one giant ripple that expands outward in all directions.

The hunters whirl around back toward us, but as the red light dwindles under their feet, they scream out. Mid-sprint, their bodies sizzle, crack and burst like human fireworks. They may as well have been vampires escaping sunlight.

Or seeking refuge under the protection of the red glow.

Damien freaks. He knocks me aside, steals the spear from the other hunter, and bolts toward Baxter. The fading wave of the red light rushes to meet him—but Damien drops to his knees, presses a palm flat against the ground. "Nenah' ka lo!" he chants, his voice hoarse and raspy. "Nenah' ka lo!"

A brilliant red circle of light pulses from under him. It explodes outward, enveloping the RV park in a brighter, more intense shade of red.

Baxter smacks the ground again, shouts, "No'h kala no'h koloh!"

and worms his way back toward the porch. The red light once again fading back outward—

"NENAH' KA LO!" Damien shrieks as he closes in, feet thundering across the ground like horse hooves. Dirt kicking up in his wake.

The red glow reignites.

As Baxter pulls himself onto the porch.

Damien skids to a halt. Cocks back the arm that's holding the spear.

Baxter reaches up toward the handle on the front door. Mutters, "No'h kala no'h—"

The spear rips through the air. Pegs Baxter's hand against the door. He screams in agony.

If not for the gang of hunters still hanging with me, this would've been as good a time as any to take off running. But I'd never make it. I'm outnumbered and still reeling from Jim's beating, among other things.

Damien joins Baxter on the porch. "Figured that would shut you up," he says as he unpins Baxter and retrieves the spear. Damien turns back to us, barks something out in Kenneh'wah, and the group of hunters escorts me toward the trailer. Meantime, I can't stop worrying about Kylie. How things have suddenly changed. The rules of Baxter's game have changed, even to his surprise. Seems Damien has learned a lot more than anyone could have expected. Especially Baxter.

Perhaps Baxter's game inadvertently granted the Kenneh'wah a wild card. Someone viler than himself. Someone who needed a way to channel his anguish. And by bringing Damien here, Baxter has unintentionally helped supply the kid with enough supernatural ammunition to spread the hostility and violence that has tainted these grounds.

Damien said it best.

He is the dynamite.

I can only guess what this power-hungry, angst-ridden kid has planned after he's done with us.

As we approach, Baxter wails and cradles his bloodied hand. "How?" he mumbles. His face frosty white with fear. "How are you all walking around in daylight?"

Damien thumbs the necklace.

Baxter gasps. "Where did you get that?" Spittle sprays out from his mouth as he says, "That's mine!"

"Then you should've been wearing it," Damien answers with a wicked grin.

"It was in my safe!"

"Wasn't safe enough."

"And the protection spell?" The remaining color drains from Baxter's face. His lower lip quivers as he asks, "How did you break that? Who taught you that chant?"

"Mac." Damien chuckles. "Can't trust anybody these days, huh?"

Baxter's gaze falls to his hand. He's bleeding profusely. If Damien doesn't kill him, the wound just might. Though something tells me the former is a lot more likely, given Damien's track record.

"I think these woods got to him," Damien says. "Can you blame him?" Damien turns to one of the hunters and gestures for his tomahawk.

Baxter shakes his head. "So now what?" All of this is sinking in, an anchor of horrifying reality. "What's your plan, stud? You just going to kill me and take over the game?"

"Fuck your game." Damien kneels next to Baxter and says very pointedly, "Me and my new family here are going to hunt down every piece of shit on this planet who screwed with me. Gonna wreck their lives. And when we're done with them, we'll do whatever we want. Go wherever we want." He grabs a handful of Baxter's hair again, yanks his head back, and brings the bone knife close to Baxter's face. "We're gonna spread like cancer."

Baxter's eyes swell to the size of golf balls as Damien rises, brings the knife up above his head.

Baxter lifts his good arm up to shield his face. "NO, PLEASE—"

Damien brings down the bone knife, cracking open Baxter's skull with one swift blow. The old man goes limp, and I feel my chest tighten.

I know I'm next.

29

Darkness on the Edge of Power

Baxter's dead body slumps forward. Damien kneels and scalps him. He hops off the porch and approaches me, tossing Baxter's scalp aside as if it were a handful of weeds.

The red glow lights the underside of Damien's face. The sunlight exposes the vertical lines of dried blood and mascara.

If Satan were a mime, it'd be this kid.

"Sorry," Damien says flatly. "We keep getting interrupted."

I'm kicked from behind, legs buckling. Once again, I'm forced down onto my knees.

Damien grabs my head and glares down at me. "You're lucky I've got shit to do." He brings the knife up to the thin skin of my forehead. "So, we'll just make this quick—"

There's a loud, angry hiss above me. Followed by an explosion that hits Damien's chest. He releases me, screaming, as he swats away at the sparks erupting from his body.

Damien's been hit with a flare. He goes berserk, arms whipping about. He screams out in the Kenneh'wah tongue to the other hunters, gesturing wildly for them to head toward the woods.

Amid the chaos, I yank the hunter's hand off my shoulder, and in one swift motion, I rise, scoop up his body under mine, and throw him over me. I hear a bone snap, and the hunter cries out. I drop my knee onto his windpipe, crushing it. He lets out a muffled cry, but he's not done yet. Out of the corner of my eye, I catch him fishing out a bone knife—but I plant my other knee into the inside of his elbow, pinning him down. His grip weakens, I steal the knife from him and stab him repeatedly until he stops moving.

I slide off him and get to my feet. My knees are wobbly. Lungs heaving. Heart pounding. The adrenaline coursing through me is cranked up to eleven.

I could probably lift a car right now.

Damien rolls on the ground, caking himself with dirt and mud, desperately trying to calm the flames. It works. But by the time he spots me, I'm standing above him. I drive my foot into his chin, knocking him flat on his back. I grasp the necklace and rip it off him.

"NOOOOOOOO!" Damien's shrill scream makes him sound like a girl. He tries to get to his feet, but I land a foot on his torso and kick him back down. I put all my body weight on that one leg, anchoring him in place, grinding into the still sizzling flesh of his chest.

"Game over," I say as I shake the necklace, "you twisted little shit."

Damien seethes. Spit spraying from his mouth as he says, "That's mine!"

"Not anymore."

I hear a woman crying out, fighting for her life.

Kylie!

I turn to see her ushered toward us by several hunters. Arms pinned behind her back. Spears and knives aimed at her as the group moves toward us.

They're also carrying the scalps of what I'm guessing are the remains of Baxter's men.

"Well lookie here," Damien nods toward the group as they approach. "Seems we've finally caught that cotton candy–haired bitch." To the approaching hunters, he utters a few phrases in Kenneh'wah. To me, eyes fuming with hate, he says, "Get off me."

Reluctantly I remove my foot and step back.

Damien grimaces and hops to his feet. The skin on his chest is a mixture of charcoal, singed flesh, and gore. It matches his head. He gestures for Kylie and the group to come close. He plants his face in her crotch and sniffs her as if she were a rose.

Kylie knees him in the face. Damien stumbles backward, laughing. A trickle of blood seeps from his nose. He touches it, looks at it, then to her. "You're spunky."

"You're a sicko."

"True." Damien shrugs. "Girls like you never look in my direction." Then his eyes light up as he advances on her. Brings his face close to hers. "But that shit's gonna change." He runs a finger down the bridge of her nose, and she turns away in disgust.

"Hey, Rupert!" I shout.

Damien spins on his heels, eyes ablaze now. "IT'S DAMIEN!"

I hold up the necklace. "Touch her again, and I'll spread your precious teeth like seeds."

"Do that," Damien says with a snarl, "and I'll slice a smile across her neck!"

"You're such a wannabe, Damien!" Kylie shouts.

"Me?" Damien points at himself. "A wannabe?" He laughs as he exchanges looks with the Kenneh'wah. Their stoic expressions never change. "I don't wannabe anything anymore." His eyes flash. "I am something."

"Yeah," Kylie says as she struggles against her captors. "A creep. A weirdo. A freak!"

"Aww, come on, Rainbow Brite." Damien backs away, tilts his head to the side as he studies her. "You know you like the attention."

"Touch me again, and I'll show you some attention."

He closes in. Grabs a handful of her hair. "I'm sure that's not the first time you've said that."

"Rupert!" I shout. "I told you not to touch her!"

Damien looks back at me. Eyes like wildfires. "MY NAME IS DAMIEN—"

Kylie jams her knee into his nuts. He doubles over.

"Yooooooou stupid bitch!" He rises back up and grabs her face. "I live for pain. And once you join me, you'll understand." He pushes her away.

"I'd rather die first," she says.

"Well, that's the plan." Damien looks back at me, skin gleaming with sweat and blood. He extends his grimy hand. "Now give me the fucking necklace."

"Let her go!" I say.

"No."

I start to slide the teeth off the necklace.

Damien puts out both hands, palms facing me. Eyes wide. "Wait!" I pause.

"You want her?" he asks.

I say nothing, knowing full well he knows I do.

"Toss down the necklace"—Damien nods toward the patch of dirt between us—"and I'll let her go."

"No."

Damien looks in my direction. "Why?"

"Because I don't trust you," I say. "And instead, I'm willing to die in her place."

"Rodney—" Kylie protests, but Damien presses a finger to her lips. To me, he says, "Go on."

"Fight me," I say without flinching.

Damien pauses. Mulls over my words.

"Fight me," I say, "without your necklace, you little pussy."

"What'd you call me?" Damien approaches me with a scowl on his face.

"You heard me. I know you're afraid." I say this though I feel the same trembling fear inside of me. The fear that I might lose.

That I don't know Damien's strength.

That I don't have enough strength of my own.

"We're doing this on my terms. Fight me." I nod toward Kylie. "And if I win, she and I both go free. You win, she's all yours."

"Ohhhh no-no-no-no!" Damien waves a finger at me. "I can do whatever the hell I want. You don't get to bargain with me."

I exchange looks with the hunters, their eyes studying me with equal interest. I tell them, "Your boy here is scared shitless. Only a real leader accepts a challenge. Do you want to be led by a man? Or by a pussy?"

"HEY!" Damien stomps his foot. Snaps his fingers at me, bringing my attention back to him. "They can't understand you, dumbass—"

"JEK NA TOK NAWAHKA!" a voice booms from the RV.

Damien freezes in place.

Everyone turns to look.

Baxter is on his feet. Damien spins around and just watches him for a beat. The petrified, reanimated remains of Damien's corpse brain realizing that he forgot Baxter would come back.

"They understood that," Baxter says with a wicked grin. "I just told them that you've been challenged—"

"I know what you said!" Damien screams. Here he was, so wrapped up in dealing with Kylie and I, the little prick forgot to tie up the one loose end.

Baxter.

To prevent that one loose end from coming back.

"Gosh, it feels good to stand up," Baxter says with a stretch and a sigh. "I'm sure my legs aren't the only part of me that's working again."

"You!" Damien screeches.

"Whoops. Guess you forgot that I'd come back?"

"Slipped my mind in all the excitement. But no biggie." Damien advances toward Baxter—but the other hunters jump between them, spears and weapons raised. "The fuck are you all doing?" He takes a step back. "You all follow me!"

Damien repeats the phrase in their tongue, but the hunters hold their ground.

"That's not how it works," Baxter says. "I've known about the

Kenneh'wah since long before you took your first breath of air. They don't respect you just because you're their substitute leader. They respect you because you're a warrior who can defend his people. Who can take on any challenger." Baxter's gaze falls on me. "And now that Rodney is holding the necklace, he's challenged you. You must either accept the challenge or die."

Damien's gaze shifts from hunter to hunter.

Baxter points at him. "Are you willing to fight for your tribe?"

Damien makes fists. Grinds his teeth and stomps his foot. "This is bullshit!"

"No, it's not bullshit," Baxter says. "It is the way it is. The way of the Kenneh'wah. Now go on, chief." Baxter nods to me, a gleam of satisfaction in his eyes. "Fight him."

Damien groans as if he's upset that he has to do chores. "All right! Fine!" He turns back to me. "Let's make this quick." He marches toward me, that hate-fire burning in his eyes. But a spear aimed at his throat stops him short.

"Nek tha, nah la, jo la ke!" a hunter tells Damien in a deep voice. The hunter then offers me his tomahawk. Gestures with a stern nod for me to take it. I do. Then I shove the necklace into my pocket. Tuck the bone knife into one of my belt loops.

Damien whips out a tomahawk as well. Arms up in a guarded position.

Here it goes.

I guess the undead still believe in a fair fight.

Or at least a man-to-man challenge.

30

The Quick and the Dead

Damien roars and charges straight at me. His lips are pulled back, glowing fangs exposed. His eyes big, bright, and boiling with malice. Tough to believe that in a mere twenty-four hours he went from a rebellious teenager with a shitty attitude to a supernatural powder keg of aged torment and adolescent rebellion.

Doesn't matter.

Either way, I'm going to rid the world of this teen menace once and for all.

Damien makes a wide lunge with his tomahawk. I duck as he throws all his weight into the swing. He spirals out of control. I drive the eye of my tomahawk into his chin as if nailing his jaw to his skull. There's a loud thwap, followed by a grunt as he's sent stumbling backward.

Behind us, the hunters shout and chant. Not sure if they're cheering for him or me.

I take a swipe at Damien's kneecap from the side, shattering it as if it's made of porcelain. Damien screams and drops to the ground quicker than I expected.

"FUUUUUUCK!" Damien wraps his hands around his leg. "FUC-CCK!" He closes his eyes, reeling in pain.

You'd think that someone missing half of their scalp would be in constant agony, and a broken kneecap wouldn't add that much more to the pain equation—but perhaps Damien only feels "new" pain?

Or maybe he's just equal parts in pain and pissed.

Who knows?

Who cares?

Doesn't stop me.

I take another swing and connect with the side of his face. The bones in his skull cave in. He drops to the ground. I kick and stomp on him as though he's a giant roach that I'm trying to crush the life out of. The glow from his teeth is now dulled by a mouthful of blood. His eyes swell. He cries out with every blow.

"I thought you said you live for pain," I say, and he gurgles in response. I bring my leg back for one final punt to his face.

A spear tip aimed at my throat stops me short.

"Nok ohla ka," a hunter says.

"What?" I ask breathlessly.

"He said back off," Baxter tells me, then kneels next to Damien. "You're nothing but a pathetic kid."

Damien pushes out several broken teeth with his tongue. His mouth looks more like a mortal wound than something he used to eat with. His words are garbled, almost inaudible, but still, he manages to mutter, "I'm . . . not . . . done."

"Then . . ." Baxter backs away and gestures for the hunters to do the same. "Continue!"

Damien pushes himself unsteadily to his feet. He sticks his fingers in his mouth and yanks out several more teeth as if they are now a useless nuisance. He takes up an odd stance, propping one hand behind his back and points his tomahawk at me with the other.

"After I kill you . . ." Damien tells me as blood seeps from his nose and mouth, "Baxter's next. Followed by Rainbow Brite." He smacks his chest. "Who I'm going to make my bitch."

"Go to hell!" Kylie screams.

I grip the tomahawk so tight you'd think it was fused to my skin.

I'm ready to end this kid. Before Damien can say another word, I race toward him, swing for his head and miss. He counters, slicing the air just inches from my face. He misses but still catches me with his other hand. The hand he kept hidden from me.

With one swift motion, Damien shoves something sharp right up into my abdomen.

I push off him and back away, staring down at hilt of a bone knife protruding from my stomach.

He got me.

My world becomes a blur of pain and panic.

That little shit got me.

Damien swings again with the tomahawk, but I catch his wrist. His expression: surprise then anger. Our eyes lock as he grimaces, struggling over control of the tomahawk. With one swift motion, I whip my body around, extend his wrist, prop myself up under him, and toss him over my back. Damien lands hard. I still haven't let go of his hand. The side of his torso is now up against my leg, secured in an arm-bar. He stares up at me, gaze shifting from the bone knife then to me. Smiling with a mouthful of blood, says, "I'm not afraid to die."

"At this point"—I rip the knife out of my gut—"neither am I." I stuff the jagged weapon into Damien's ear. He barely lets out a whimper as his body goes limp in my arms.

The violent glow in his eyes fades to black.

Out of the corner of my eye, I catch a glimpse of Baxter just as he slams into me, knocking me off my feet. For a split-second I'm weightless. Then my jaw crunches and my head rattles as I do a backward swan dive onto the dirt.

"This is my game," Baxter says.

Kylie screams out my name.

The hunters begin to chant in unison.

I barely have enough energy and stamina to lift up my head. Feels as though there's an invisible fist pinning me against the earth.

"You think I'm going to let you or this piece of shit here take over?" Baxter removes the bone knife from Damien's skull and aims it at me.

"Not a chance."

The chanting grows louder.

"Rodney! Come on!" Kylie cries. "Get-up-get-up-get-up!"

The hunters take a step forward, tightening their circle around us.

Baxter brings up his foot to stomp me out like a spent cigarette—but I reach up, grab it, and push him backward. Using every ounce of remaining stamina that I have, I get to my feet, though I'm wobbly as a top.

Baxter comes at me, making several jabs with the bone knife. I throw up my arms to protect myself, but the blows slice me from my wrists to my elbows. My arms feel as if they're on fire. He lands a kick square at the knife wound in my gut. I let out a pained groan and lunge clumsily forward to try to grab his knife hand, but in my uncoordinated state, I miss completely.

There's a flash of motion, Baxter brings the knife up under me, which is followed by a sharp pain in my chest. In my heart to be exact.

Baxter backs away and observes my reaction.

Watches me stare down in horror as the previous scene is repeated, only instead of the knife hilt protruding from my gut, it's now sticking out from my chest.

The pain . . .

Unlike anything I've ever experienced.

Can't breathe . . .

Can't think . . .

I look at Kylie . . .

Her eyes exploding with tears as she screams like a mad woman.

Since I can't speak, I instead shoot her a look that says . . .

I'm sorry.

31

Of Musk & Sugar

At first, there's the gentle sound of a stream. Then birds chirping. A warm breeze brushes against my skin. Crisp spring air fills my lungs. Honeysuckle. Wildflowers and . . .

A woman.

A distinct perfume of musk and sugar.

I open my eyes and gaze up at a crystal blue sky.

Is this heaven?

An arm slides across my chest, and I nearly jump. Baxter?

Not hardly.

An exotic, olive-skinned woman with hair as black as the feathers of a crow mounts me. I feel her wriggle and grind her groin against mine—

I push her off. "Who the hell are you?"

She rolls her eyes, giggles playfully, and brings up her hand to caress my cheek. She smells wonderful.

"Nannokto," she says with a smile. "Where did you go?"

"What?"

"Did your dreams take you away from me?" she asks, a warm smile still on her face. "Did the strength of my magic consume you?"

"I don't know what you're talking about. I don't even know who—"

She brushes her thumb against my lips to silence me. "We should go." With her other hand, she grabs me between the legs. Rubs me furiously for a moment. "Finish this later. My father will be looking for me soon."

She then plants a kiss on my both of my eyes and rises, exposing her naked beauty to me. She is remarkably striking. Her onyx mane spills downward, reaching all the way to her hips. Her chocolate brown eyes stay fixed on me as she wraps a blanket around her body—zigzag patterns. Earth tones. Pointy symbols. Handwoven.

She carefully dresses, staring at me with a loving gaze. Her ruby lips curl into a smile as she sticks a single feather at the top of her head.

"Nannokto, tell me," she says as she clasps her hands by her heart, "if my father won't let us be together, would you be willing to leave the tribe?"

"Um . . ."

"To be with me?"

I'm still trying to assess where the heck I am and what's going on.

"The tribe would survive without us," she says. "You know that."

"O . . .K?"

She raises her hands up to the sky, genuflecting. "You know that I can call upon the spirits." She shifts her gaze back down toward me. "To watch over us. To see our love through the end. Through the eternal. Our ancestors will guide us toward our new home."

"Um . . ."

"You don't have to answer me now," she says as she tilts her head to one side. "I know it's a big decision for you."

"It is?"

In the distance—horrifying screams.

Women and children crying.

Men shouting.

Then the crackle of what sounds like . . .

Gunfire.

The olive-skinned woman turns toward the commotion, then looks back at me. The peaceful expression on her face now replaced with terror.

"Nannokto"—she extends her hand toward me—"we must go! Something's wrong!"

And just as I take her hand, I hear a distant pop and watch in horror as the side of her neck bursts open. She crashes to the ground next to me.

"Jesus!" I lean over her, cover the wound with my hands, but the blood.

There's so much blood!

She stares up at me, her eyes pleading for me to save her.

"Hang on!" I tell her. "I'm going to get us help."

Help?

Help from where?

I don't know where the hell I am!

She responds by making these awful gurgling sounds. She's choking on her own fluids. A dark red river of blood spills from her mouth.

"Nanno . . ." she utters as she brings a quivering hand to my lips. Then barely gets out the words, "I . . . love . . ."

Her hand drops.

Her head flops to the side, gaze frozen as if looking off to the horizon. The gaping hole where the bullet tore into her neck stares back at me like a bloody, wet mouth.

"God," I say with a gasp.

She's gone.

A moment ago, this beautiful woman smelled of flowers and heaven, now she reeks of blood and death. And those aren't the only smells in the air. The smell of gun smoke moves in from all directions as more men clamor in the distance.

I'm suddenly overwhelmed with the need to destroy something. Whoever killed this woman needs to taste the cold end of my—

Tomahawk.

I bring it up to my face and stare at it as if it were handed to me from God himself. As if it were something I worshipped. As if it was going to bring me salvation.

"Keyaha . . ." The name escapes my mouth on its own. Comes out in a soft whisper.

Keyaha?

Who is . . .

I mean, how do I know her . . . name?

I brush my hand against her face, her warm blood spreading across her skin like crimson mascara. "Keyaha!"

At the mention of her name, I'm overcome by a sense of loss.

I feel a bottomless hole open in my heart. A sinking feeling like nothing in this world matters anymore. Like I can no longer appreciate the blue skies, the scent of honeysuckle or the soft breeze against my skin—our skin—as we made love in secret. Away from the tribe.

Away from her father.

He never knew.

And now he'll never know—

Stop it!

I bring a hand to my forehead. Shut my eyes for a second.

What is going on? I feel like I have two brains, two parallel lines of thought in motion, two sets of emotions playing out at the same time. I feel a mixture of confusion . . .

And madness.

Keyaha.

I gently close her eyes and kiss her forehead. I start to cry. Can't believe I'm shedding tears for this woman that I don't know—

Keyaha!

I mean that I have known . . . forever...

My Keyaha.

I've always known her because I have always loved her because I am . . .

Nannokto!

"No! My name is Rodney!"

A storm of enmity stirs inside me. I squeeze my eyes tight and hold my hand against my head as if preventing it from bursting open. I must be going crazy. Maybe I'm asleep? Unconscious?

Dead . . .

Or maybe I'm in Hell—

"NANNOKTO!" a woman shouts.

A very voluptuous woman runs toward me. She's naked and drenched in blood. Someone has had their way with her. Looks as if she was attacked by a large mob—or just a rabid few. Arms outstretched. Her long hair flows behind her like a black flag as she speeds across the field toward me.

I jump up, tomahawk in hand.

"NANNOKTO!" she shouts once more.

Our eyes meet as she closes in on me. Dread all over her face. I reach out to her—

There's the snap of gunfire.

Her chest explodes. She plows into the dirt like a plane crashing into the earth.

I shout out a name—another name I don't recognize:

"LAKO'NA!"

My eyes flood with tears, but I wipe them away to catch sight of a man in the distance. He's laughing as he reloads a fire stick. The man is dressed in something I've never seen before.

He is not of my tribe.

Or one of our rivals—

STOP IT!

I shake my head. Shake off these foreign thoughts from Nannokto.

And with a clear head, I notice the man in the distance is dressed like a Spanish soldier. Circa 1500 or whatever. He's wearing one of those trademark, pointed metal helmets of the conquistadors. Chest protected in a steel shell.

Wait.

No.

He's not dressed like a Spanish soldier.

He is one.

Another soldier joins him. The two of them share a laugh as the first one raises his musket and takes aim at me—

I fling my tomahawk at him, sending it sailing end over end at his head, where it hits him dead in the nose. His helmet is knocked forward, covering his eyes. He trips over his own feet and falls. The gun goes off and pops a round in the dirt in front of me.

The second soldier fumbles to load up a crossbow.

But I'm already headed in his direction.

I leap into the air, grab him, and take him down to the ground. We roll around, and fortunately, I land on top. He's yelling at me in Spanish, arms shooting upward, trying desperately to get a hold of me, but I overpower him. I got a full tank of vengeance fueling my fire, and he's about to get cooked.

I bring down an elbow onto his nose. Part of his helmet catches my arm, slices through my skin and jams into bone. The pain is brutal, but a brief flash of Keyaha's face distracts me temporarily. Blinded by anger, I tear off his helmet and rain my fists down on his face as if it's made of pizza dough. Cartilage and bone give under the blows. Blood splatters in all directions—

Blood from the both of us.

I smash his face in.

Literally. Then climb off him and go for the other scumbag who shot my beloved Keyaha. He mutters in Spanish and spits at me as I pin his back against a tree, locking his neck with the boney side of my forearm.

I feel a blazing sharp pain my gut.

He smiles at me as I glance down. The hilt of a knife sticks from out my stomach.

Déjà vu of the worst kind.

He mumbles something else at me, chuckles, and then I surprise the crap out of him when I rip the blade out and hold it in front of his

191

THE DEATH WISH GAME

soulless eyes.

"This is for"—and her name escapes my lips once again—"Keyaha!"

I shove his knife right through his neck until I hit bark, literally nailing him to the tree.

I back away as he gurgles and slaps at his neck, trying to grab at the hilt, but it's buried so deep in his neck, that he's got no chance in hell of—

There's a sharp sensation in the center of my back—a horrific burning pain that travels throughout my entire body, followed by the sudden inability to feel my legs. I slump to the ground, and my forehead clips one of the tree roots jutting up. Something cracks. My skull perhaps? I try to reach for my head, but I can't move my legs, my arms.

Nothing.

I CAN'T MOVE!

"Keyaha!"

I don't know why I shout her name, but I do.

At least I can talk.

The air is filled with the sounds of babies, children, and women screaming their brains out. As my vision sharpens somewhat, I see a wall of flames in the distance. People scurrying back and forth. Soldiers taking aim and firing a variety of ordnance. Bodies falling to the ground.

It's a nightmare unfolding in real time.

I hear voices and laughter behind me. I try to roll over to see who's coming, but it's impossible. Might as well be made of stone since my body is not taking me anywhere. I feel the earth vibrate under my head as several Spaniards surround me. They lean over, staring down at me as if I'm some wild rabbit they have successfully trapped.

A pair of worn black leather boots swoops past my nose, nearly clipping it, as one of the soldiers steps over my head. He kneels down next to me, and I get a waft of his body odor. He smells like sewage.

He smells like the Devil.

Dried specks of blood pepper his helmet, which casts a shadow across his nose and eyes. Through his black-and-gray beard, he cracks a smile—exposing a mouthful of rotten teeth in various stages of decay. He murmurs something to me in Spanish as he produces a gold cross from around his neck. He kisses it and holds it up to the clouds for the heavens to see.

Heck of a way to spread Christianity, asshole. I'm sure Jesus did not approve your message.

I want to get to my feet and fight him but I can't.

I'm a vegetable.

The bearded soldier glances back at his comrades, says something as he points at his backside, which gets a laugh out of everyone. I took all of two years of Spanish in middle school. Not enough to figure out what they're saying. Though I do hear them say espalda several times followed by them mocking me for being unable to move.

Espalda?

Oh yeah . . .

It means back.

They shot me in the back, like a coward.

Mr. Beard here is doing most of the mocking. He storms off, his battle brothers grinning like hyenas as they watch him go. This is quickly followed by the faint and wet sounds of something being cut and ripped away; meat being stripped away from bone.

As they continue to watch their buddy do whatever it is he's doing, I try once more to move any part of my body.

Nothing.

I can barely lift my head, or raise a pinky.

Mr. Beard comes back, stares down at me with that wicked grin of his, hidden beneath a wild mess of facial hair. He dangles something in his hand like a yo-yo, then tosses it, where it lands right in front of my face.

Unfortunately, it's not a yo-yo.

It's a piece of Keyaha.

THE DEATH WISH GAME

A strip of her hair and a fleshy sliver of her scalp to be exact.

Keyaha!

My love.

Everything . . .

Goes . . .

White . . .

An atomic bomb of pure madness mushrooms inside me—

"KEYAAAAAAAHAAAAAAAAA!"

I scream her name out as tears burn my eyes, making it hard to look upon my enemies.

The very men who killed my love.

The stranger kneels and stares into my eyes. He smells of dead things and desecrated earth. He's speaking to me in the evil tongue and laughing. I want to cut that tongue from his vile dog mouth, but my body betrays me. Something has cursed my limbs.

I scream at him for taking my Keyaha, but he just laughs and says in his wicked tongue, "Yo mato animales."

I want to tear him apart, but I cannot.

"Tu comprende?" he repeatedly says in a language I have never heard before. "YO MATO ANIMALES!"

My body refuses to move. I am but prey at the mercy of these savage coyotes.

He raises up his fire stick, points it at me—

32

Two in One

There's a blast of light, and I jump to my feet, gasping as if I've just been resuscitated.

"Welcome back," a voice says.

It takes me a moment for everything to focus.

I'm surrounded by hunters.

Along with Baxter. "You took a shorter trip than most."

How am I back? Where was I? I touch where Baxter stabbed me. The gaping wound is still there. The flesh in and around it burns.

"Yeah," Baxter says, "your heart isn't working like it used to."

I'm alive?

But how?

Wait.

I'm not alive.

I'm something else.

"We still feel pain," he says, "but that pain is overshadowed by the venom inside us."

I reach for the bone knife that I had stuffed in my pants. It's gone. Along with the necklace.

"Looking for this?" Baxter asks as he puts on the necklace.

No!

He took it from me while I was . . . dead.

"Now," Baxter's voice drops several octaves, deepening as he says,

"Nannokto . . ." then, "you may come out!"

My eyes suddenly feel like they're on fire. This is followed by a ringing in my head. I squeeze my eyes shut, grit my teeth, and press my palms flat against the sides of my head. I feel as though my skull is trying to split itself in two. It's as if Baxter's words are like a concussion grenade, setting off a blast of light, blinding me to the world around me—

And as my eyes focus, I take a moment to . . .

A moment to assess my surroundings.

Assess?

What is this word—assess?

Many words are floating around in my head. The language of the strangers is woven within the dialect of my own.

I glance at my hands. Light skinned. The color of the enemy.

What is this?

Whose hands are these?

How am I here?

What happened to the men armed with their fire sticks?

What happened to Keyaha?

"Nannokto," a familiar voice says, and I glance up, recognizing three of my Kenneh'wah brothers—Okoto, Negache, Kuma. How are they here?

They have a fair-skinned woman in their possession. She is beautiful, though not nearly as lovely as my Keyaha. Okoto tells me that they have been awakened to protect our land from the invaders—from the chek-tah.

"Nannokto?" A light-skinned man with a large belly knows my name. "Mak tah, Baxter. Jekat ala no?"

This . . . man . . . Baxter . . .

He speaks our tongue?

"Jekat ala no?" Baxter repeats his question to me as he caresses the chieftain necklace draped around his neck. It is adorned with the pulled teeth of our ancestors.

I look to my brothers, one by one, searching for an answer within their glowing eyes—eyes that flicker like torches. But instead of answers, they look at me with vacant expressions. They are not themselves. They are not the vibrant brothers I remember. Their faces hang like the dead, with skin as pale as the shells of the eggs of birds and lizards.

Is this truly our new leader—a foreigner?

As if reading my thoughts, or more likely my expression, they finally nod in affirmation.

Affirmation?

What is this word—affirmation? What are many of these words inside me? These are the words of the foreigners. And yet they are words that I understand. Words that I have never spoken, yet know with such clarity. Such understanding.

Louder now, the Baxter asks me if I am with him.

I'm so confused.

"Rodney!" the chek-tah woman screams at me.

I turn to her, grab her face, and search her eyes. There's a wild flame that burns inside her. Her bones and muscles as taut as rope.

Baxter tells me to kill this chek-tah woman and tosses me his knife.

"Rodney, please!" She speaks to me in the foreign tongue.

I turn to Baxter. He makes a stabbing motion with his hand and laughs.

I look back at the chek-tah woman—

She makes a sudden move with her foot, hitting me below my stomach . . . between my legs—

A white light explodes in my brain as I keel over.

I gasp. Feels as though I've just come out of hibernation. The Kenneh'wah warriors around me look on with vapid expressions. Baxter observes me with the apathetic curiosity of a scientist watching the effects of his experiments on his subjects.

The experiment of merging the ancient dead with a modern soul.

Two personalities in one body.

This must be what Bear was going through. Fighting to keep himself, keep his psyche, intact from that primeval malevolence leaking its will and its desires into him—making its ambitions for acrimony and vengeance his own.

It just took a little pain—a solid kick to the nuts—to snap me out of it.

"Come on, Rodney," Kylie pleads as I look down at her. There's a weakness in her eyes. A pleading look that betrays her tough exterior. Her lips tremble, a glimmer of tears forming at the corners of her eyes. I bring the bone knife up to her face. "I know you're in there."

I wink at her.

She freezes.

"The game ends"—I turn to Baxter—"now!"

Baxter's face morphs from surprise to anger. He shouts out commands to the other hunters. And since I've got Nannokto's soul unexplainably intertwined with mine, I understand every Kenneh'wah word he says.

Baxter is telling the other hunters to take me down because I didn't transition over completely. That my soul is tainted.

That I'm still chek-tah.

"Akha teya noka!" The words escape my lips from somewhere deep inside me as if I've known this language all along.

But I know I haven't.

It's Nannokto, and I feel a gnawing in my head, like an impending migraine. It's as if his spirit is trying to push his way back into my psyche.

If I lose my sanity to Nannokto, there's a chance I may not come back. And Kylie will most likely die by my own hands. I must make this quick.

"Akha teya noka!" I repeat to the others that I'm challenging Baxter.

The hunters respond by telling Baxter he must accept the challenge or be killed himself—rules he already knows.

Baxter shoots them a dirty look. To me, "So this is the thanks I get for sparing you from your pathetic former life?" Baxter grabs a tomahawk from one of the hunters.

"Yeah, and in return, I'm going to spare you from yours."

Baxter takes a deep breath, snarls. "You won't return a second time."

"Guess we'll see."

Baxter raises his tomahawk in the air, and we charge each other.

33

Mato Animales

Like two semis colliding at eighty miles an hour, Baxter and I slam into each other. He's no longer stronger than I am since I'm now powered by the paranormal vigor of the Kenneh'wah.

I raise the knife and bring it down on him—but Baxter stops me short, locking both arms under me. His eyes pulse like red warning lights as he lands a kick to my chest. I'm knocked backward. He follows with a swing of his tomahawk. I duck, just barely missing the broad arc of the weapon. I step in, and with one quick jab, I stab him just below his rib cage. He growls as he whirls around, and the cold stone of his tomahawk clips my chin.

My hands break my fall. I roll away just as Baxter smacks his tomahawk against the ground where it lands with a thud. I drive my heel into his kneecap, hitting it sideways. He roars, buckles, and shifts his weight to one side like a bridge that's lost one of its supports. He grabs his knee. A wildfire blazing in his eyes as he says, "Nannokto, nela kalah!"

Which means . . .

Nannokto . . .

Come out . . .

There's a flash of white light. I grab my head, hands clutching either side as if preventing it from exploding.

I rub my eyes.

Rise to my feet.

Baxter has one knee on the ground, the other he clutches with his hand. His eyes are the color of blood moons. In a voice that's as firm as the land we walk on, he tells me to sacrifice myself because I have gone mad. "Joka!" he barks at me like a wild dog. "Joka! Joka! Joka!" Now! Now! Now!

He pulls the knife from out his side and then tosses it at my feet. "Joka!" Now!

I glare at the weapon as if it is a dead bird.

"Joka, Nannokto!"

I look to the others and ask them, "Have I gone crazy? Is there a chek-tah spirit poisoning my soul? Clouding my being?" But before they respond, Baxter leaps up and swings his tomahawk. Hits me—

White light.

An explosion of burning pain.

I drop to my knees.

Eyes fluttering, I awaken to find Baxter staring down at me.

Where the hell did I just go? What is going on? I feel as if I've been slipping in and out of a coma.

"I don't need an unstable guy like you around if you're not going to be a part of something bigger than yourself," Baxter says. "However, that's always been your problem, right?"

The side of my face feels wet. I touch it to find it's covered in blood. The blood is gooier than I would've expected.

But then again, I died.

Right?

"As the shaman once told me," Baxter goes on, "Nannokto had a lot of unresolved anger. He was quite the warrior in his day." He wobbles as he walks, knees clicking with each step. "Pity he was reincarnated into your lousy body." He turns toward the hunters, asks for a spear so that he can finish me, and one is thrown in his direction.

I try to get to my feet, but Baxter just kicks me back down. He raises the spear up above me.

"Maybe this will bring Nannokto out of you," he says.

"Not if you kill me again."

With a shit-eating grin, Baxter winks at me. He takes a step back and launches the spear over my head.

I hear a wet thump.

Quickly followed by a piercing scream.

I push myself off the ground and turn to find Kylie with the spear protruding from her chest. She dangles in the hunters' arms, struggling to free herself. Blood spills from her lips and flowers out from out her wound as she locks eyes with me . . .

Then her head slumps forward.

"KYLIE!" Hate and hysteria overwhelm me.

Baxter nonchalantly dusts his hands off. "Who said I was going to kill you?"

There's a flash of light in my mind again. I wince and when I open my eyes . . .

Kylie . . . is . . . moving . . .

Several more flashes of light blind me temporarily, and when they stop, I find I'm no longer staring at Kylie, but another woman—the exotic woman . . .

Keyaha.

Her face flickers momentarily. A single frame on a film reel. Just one twenty-fourth of a second, and then Kylie's face reappears.

And then it repeats.

Keyaha.

Kylie.

Keyaha.

Kylie.

Keyaha.

She looks at me with eyes as infinite and bottomless as black holes ready to swallow me into them forever.

"Nannokto," Keyaha says, "come back to me."

"No—"

A flash of light.

Followed by a stabbing sensation . . .

I blink several times, and a beautiful woman comes into focus. It's—

"Keyaha!"

She smiles at me. Her face half covered in blood. They've speared her like some wild boar. Why have they done this to her?

Okoto retrieves the spear and then tosses her body aside.

I jump to my feet, a hundred pains cry out from my body—a chorus of misery—but all that is nothing compared to what is tearing apart my heart. With the swiftness of a coyote, I pounce on Okoto—my old friend.

My brother!

And now he dares aim his spear at me?

"Nyek koh la!" I didn't do this, he says. And then he tells me to look at Keyaha once more.

She lies on her side, and as I roll her over I find that she is not Keyaha—but that chek-tah woman!

What is this?

Is this shaman trickery?

Why did I just see my Keyaha, but now she has the face of the chek-tah?

I ask Okoto if I did this. Did I kill this woman?

He says no.

Then I ask him who did, and he points the spear at Baxter.

Our new chieftain.

"Nannokto?" Baxter then asks if I have returned.

"Returned from where?" I ask him.

Baxter chuckles, tells me not to worry about that and says he's glad to have me back because he needs me.

I gaze at the dead chek-tah woman at my feet.

Why do I feel as though I have been in and out of a dream?

Baxter tells me that she is nothing more than a chek-tah. Not even worthy of a pig's burial. He then asks me to call off the challenge so we can move on.

Challenge?

I tell him I did not issue a challenge, but he insists that I call if off anyway, that I completely surrender to him as chieftain. Surrender and he will command the other Kenneh'wah to spare me. He will tell them that the chek-tah spirit—the one who wrongfully issued the challenge—has been purged from my being.

His words feel wrong.

Everything feels wrong.

This light-skinned man—Baxter—is foul. The air around him reeks of deceit.

I look to my brothers. Having never called off a challenge, I'm not sure what comes next. Okoto reminds us all that a challenge may never be issued twice. If I call it off, I may not challenge the same man a second time.

"Nannokto!" Baxter shouts my name and urges me to withdraw.

I feel I have been woken up in the wrong time. To witness the death of my beautiful Keyaha once more, whether through trickery or through my own insanity.

I am confused. Why have I been awakened?

Okoto presses me to call off the challenge . . .

Or finish the fight.

I kneel next to the chek-tah woman. Her face is so familiar.

"Answer me!" Baxter speaks in words similarly foreign, like those of the light-skinned strangers who took my Keyaha from me.

Perhaps he is one of the foreigners who slaughtered us. He has traveled through time to kill my beloved once again before my eyes, proclaimed himself leader, and manipulated the souls of my people. And yet he dares ask that I would be a part of his wickedness?

"This punk kid here actually had a good idea." Baxter seems consumed with the sound of his own voice, savoring his own madness as he speaks to himself, for I know my brothers do not understand him. "We could spread like cancer. A never-ending, recycling horde of hate." He licks his lips, eyes pulsing.

My brothers may be afraid or honoring the tradition of respecting the holder of the gem'kah, but I am no fool. This light-skinned man is the real chek-tah. He is not Kenneh'wah, even if he is holding the teeth of our forefathers as if they are his. Nor does he deserve the honor of leading our tribe.

Baxter takes a step forward. "Ha no lok takano?" What is my decision?

I decide that he is a wolf disguised as one of us.

I decide that he must die because he is chek-tah.

I yank the spear from Okoto's grip and recall the words spoken to me many moons ago. "Yo mato animales."

"Perro feo!" Baxter responds in his devil tongue.

I raise the spear. His eyes widen in surprise—before he can move, I launch it at him, catching him right in his stomach. He screams and keels over, clutching the end of the spear in his hand. I charge at him, ready to tear his flesh from his bones. Though as I make my way toward him, he chuckles and looks up at me with those demon eyes.

I am almost upon him, going to rip that grin from his lips—

There's the sound of something snapping. Then a blur of movement. Baxter suddenly jumps up like a fox pouncing on his prey.

That prey being me.

And the moment my hands touch his shoulders, his hands reach out, and with the strength of a black bear, he pulls me into him—into the jagged end of the spear protruding from his gut. The wooden shaft of the spear sinks into my stomach as he pins me tight against him. Shock takes over. I feel this foreign body I'm trapped in giving out.

I try to push away from Baxter, but he holds me tight. He moves one hand behind his back. I hear wood snap as he breaks off the end of the spear. "Tenias razon. Mato animales." He laughs and then says, "Perdoname."

He then says in our language that I was right.

That he kills . . . animals.

205

Yes, I recognize that venomous tongue of his, the tone of his poisonous words. He is of the foreigners!

Fighting through my pain, I reach up and choke him, but he only seems to feed off this, and the burning of his demon eyes grows. His smile stretches. He brings his arm up behind my head and shoves something into the side of my neck. Instantly I release him, and he laughs as he pushes me away, freeing me from the spear and his deadly embrace. I land hard on my back. I try desperately to pull the weapon from my neck.

What did he get me with?

Baxter laughs louder now. I flop to one side and catch him pulling out the spear from his belly as if it were a mere splinter. He holds it up like a sacred artifact. "Got you," he says.

Seems he broke off the tip of the spear and stuck me with it.

I can no longer speak.

Can't even scream.

I feel my energy draining.

My vision fading.

Baxter tosses the broken spear shaft aside and says, "Adios, Nan-nokto. Could've used your help." He raises his shoulders up and down. "But I guess we'll be carrying on without you." He turns his back on me, approaches my brothers, and snatches a tomahawk from one of them.

A chek-tah has defeated me.

Again.

Given this second chance at revenge, another opportunity to avenge the death of my Keyaha and my people, I have failed once more. And now he will lead my brothers to continue the wicked deeds of the foreigners. To kill in the name of the wolves. The very pigs who slaughtered us in life will now lead us in death.

I want to continue the fight. I am not afraid.

I try to push myself off the ground, but my body falters. I feel myself slipping once more into the dark slumber.

No!

I must fight it.

I yank the spear tip out from my neck. But I am too late. The call of death stiffens me, and I unwillingly submit to it—

But not before I hear the shrill cry of a woman.

34

Hell Hath No Fury

My head falls to one side. I catch sight of the chek-tah woman screaming. Her eyes glowing as blue as a cloudless afternoon sky. She examines her arms as if gazing upon them for the first time.

"Yatah la chek-tah." She says that she bears the skin color of a chek-tah.

Okoto and the others look at her as if watching a delirious cat awaken from a nap.

The woman looks in my direction. "Nannokto?" She runs to my side, drops to her knees and places a hand gently on my forehead. "Nannokto, koalka nah'tal." She tells me not to leave her. Then tells me that she is my . . .

Keyaha!

My eyes deceive me as she appears very much as this chek-tah woman and not my beloved Keyaha. But it's as if she is reading my thoughts. She leans close to me, whispers in my ear that I never answered her question—the question she asked just before dying at the hands of the foreigners and their cursed fire sticks.

Would I be willing to leave the tribe for her?

This is her.

My Keyaha.

I want to tell her yes—yes, I would leave for her. I would do anything for her!

I try to respond, to even say her name, but the only thing that comes from my mouth is blood.

"You're too late to save him," Baxter says.

Tears fall from her eyes as her gaze levels with mine. Her face blurs as the cold grip of death reaches once more into my soul.

"Nannokto!" she shouts as she shakes me, trying to keep me awake in this world.

"Kiss him goodbye already," Baxter says as he comes into view, standing over the two of us like an evil giant. "You two make me want to puke."

She leans in close once again. Whispers that she won't let my dreams take me away from her again. Nor will she let this chek-tah break us apart.

That her magic will consume me.

That her magic will consume us all.

She tells me this, all the while never lifting her hand from my forehead, which suddenly grows hot. I want to scream out in pain, but all that comes out is a whimper.

"Enough!" Baxter tears Keyaha off me and pushes her aside. "We killed your boyfriend hundreds of years ago. And you know what they say? History has a way of repeating itself." He brings up the tomahawk—

But Keyaha moves so fast, even Baxter is caught off guard. She grabs his wrists and stops him from delivering the final blow. The color of Keyaha's eyes changes from blue to yellow. Her entire body does the same. It is as if she is on fire.

"Jot ko la noa!" Baxter tells her she can't turn on him. He is the chieftain now. He commands my brothers to attack her. They respond by raising their spears and stepping forward—but she spins around and aims a fiery hand in their direction.

"Soelka Keyaha Lokota, peoska na Tekano Lokota." She tells them that she is Keyaha Lokota, daughter of Tekano Lokota—our real chief. Her eyes sparkle like flames from a pit. She then asks how dare they take aim at her and not challenge this chek-tah snake who raped their wives and slaughtered their children?

Our wives.

Our children.

My brothers exchange confused looks. Then hang their heads in shame. Keyaha goes on to tell them that this chek-tah, Baxter, has the necklace, but he does not have the heart of the tribe. He is the false leader.

Baxter squirms and tries to move but is paralyzed by her grip. A rat in the talons of an eagle. He calls out to Keyaha, challenging her to try to take his authority from him.

An immense pain—like that of a thousand daggers stabbing—consumes me. I clench my jaw, shut my eyes—

There's a flash of white light.

I open my eyes as if waking from a nightmare of violence, suffering, and blood. A montage of images cycles through my mind. Glimmers of fighting, bloodshed, death. Fragments of the Kenneh'wah language echoing in my head like a long-distance phone call with a bad signal. As I come to, I realize that most of those glimmers, those flashes of brutality and bloodshed, are all still very much right here in my head.

It isn't a dream or an abstract nightmare, but the horrible truth.

Kylie is holding Baxter's wrists. She brings them down to his side then turns back to look at me. Her entire body, from her head to her toes, is ablaze with a yellow light. She's a walking fireball.

I feel a sharp pain in the side of my neck. I wince and reach for it—but I can't move my arms!

Kylie!

I try to say her name but all that comes out is a liquid that I can only surmise is a mixture of blood and spit and my definitive death.

I'm going to pass at any moment.

I try to utter her name once more, but can't.

"Fight me, you stupid bitch!" Baxter barks. "Don't just hold my hands. Fight me if you think you deserve to take control of these feather heads."

Kylie turns pale. She turns back to Baxter. "I don't need to fight you. I don't need to control them." She eyes the other hunters. "I want them to have peace. The peace the two evils inside of your soul have stolen and held captive for years."

"If peace is what you want, then come and get it!" Baxter leans forward, eyes burning with an almost neon red glow. "Vamos, puta!"

Kylie plants her hand square on Baxter's face, palm dead center on his nose, fingers splayed open. A white light escapes from beneath her grip, casting a creepy light over his entire face. He cries out. His screams growing louder by the second.

Mid scream, she breaks away, steps back and tells Baxter, "You stay right there."

Baxter does.

Seems she has somehow locked him in place. Hit the pause button on his pain. His face is frozen into a sort of permanent scream. The red glow from his eyes fades. His eyeballs are the only things that he has control over now. They shift from side to side, watching Kylie make her way from one hunter to another as if taking roll call.

Somehow Kylie is speaking to them in the Kenneh'wah tongue. As she walks up to each one of the hunters. They bow as she touches their foreheads. The same bright white light emanates from their heads, travels up her arm in a ring of light, and fades once it reaches her scalp. Then the hunter collapses. She moves around the tribe and does this until every one of the hunters is on the ground.

Baxter's eyes swell as she approaches him, unsure of what she's about to do next. A weak groan escapes his throat. Mouth still hung open, he looks like a baby chick awaiting its mother's offering.

Something tells me that what Kylie is about to feed him isn't food.

Kylie places a hand on his forehead. Baxter's groaning gets louder. A waterfall of tears slides down his cheeks.

"You want forever?" she asks him, tilting her head to the side. "Well, how about an eternity of pain and misery?"

Her hand glows once more on his forehead, and he screams the way a man would if he were plummeting down an elevator shaft to his death.

"I want both of your souls to have back all of the pain," she says. "Pain you inflicted onto the Kenneh'wah and onto those you wrongfully deemed as chek-tah."

Blood pours out of Baxter's nose as his entire body shakes. It's almost as if she's electrocuting him. But she's not. She's giving him what he always wanted, what he's coveted.

The agony and suffering of innocents.

The white light intensifies until there's a blinding explosion. I close my eyes. When I open them, Baxter is lying on the ground trembling and twitching like a dying fish. Kylie stands above him, watching on.

"Congratulations. Their pain is now your pain." She spits on him. "Now the Kenneh'wah can finally rest in peace, and you get to enjoy an eternity of misery." She leans over and tears the necklace from his neck. "And I'll make sure this gets to the right person."

Baxter's body twitches sporadically, wriggling as if some latent electric current still pulses through him. Kylie kneels next to him, plants a hand on his head. Her hand emits a brief flash of white and then his head flops to one side.

"You're going to need all the rest you can get," she whispers to him. "Because when you awaken, you'll know Hell."

An unexplainable warmth washes over me. I close my eyes as I feel my body give out and the last thing I hear is Kylie's voice calling out, "Rodney!"

35

Trucks and Mojitos

The afterlife sounds an awful lot like a truck.

The ride is a lot bumpier than I expected, too. When I come to, I nearly jump out of my skin. This is not a tunnel of light leading to Heaven. Or, worse, a pit toward the bowels of Hell. Seems the road to the afterlife is traveled via a Ford pickup . . .

Driven by Kylie?

"Morning!" she says to me with a big grin. She lifts a finger off the wheel, points it up at the sky. "Well, technically it's almost dinner time."

It's just her and me in the truck. No Baxter. No Damien. No Kenneh'wah.

Is this another dream?

Am I lying dead in the middle of a field, in the middle of Baxter's jungle?

Difficult to tell what's real any more, considering what my mind has been through.

I touch my neck. No gash. No blood. Perfectly healed.

I shoot Kylie a baffled look.

"You were snoring," she says with a chuckle.

I look down at my chest. I'm wearing a UCF T-shirt.

"I think Baxter stole that from one of his victims," she tells me. "He didn't strike me as the literary type. Not to mention that shirt's a medium." She taps her belly. "Baxter wasn't exactly a fit guy."

I lift the shirt. Check for wounds. Not a scratch on me. "Kylie—"

Oh my God!

I can talk.

My vocal chords work. The hauntingly distinct feeling of trying to communicate with a mouth full of blood is no longer my reality.

"Yessssss?" she says.

"What's going on?"

"Well, we're headed for Miami." She glances at me out of the corner of her eye. Winks as she says, "Got to finish the trip we started after all, right?"

"Miami?" I repeat the word as if it's completely foreign.

"Yep." She pats the steering wheel. "And we're headed there courtesy of Baxter's F250." She cranks up the air conditioning. "God, I've missed AC."

I simply nod, trying to take this all in. Along the roadside, a wall of pine trees and palm trees zip by as the sun settles to the west just above them. "Kylie, what happened to my wounds?" I turn to her. "I thought I died."

"You almost did. A second time, I might add."

"Yeah, but . . . I should've died."

"Right." Kylie shrugs. "But we saved you."

"We?"

"Keyaha and I." She taps at her temple. "She might have been at the steering wheel in my mind, but she kept me in the driver's seat with her. My thoughts were her thoughts and vice versa."

"So . . . she possessed you?"

"More like channeled."

"Oh yeah. Human radios. As your sister used to say, right?" I detect the echoes of a headache forming in the back of my neck. My body feels as if I've just survived a car crash. Throbbing everywhere. It hurts to move. It hurts to be alive.

But at least I am alive.

"Keyaha inhabited me only temporarily." Kylie glances in my direction. "She needed someone like me to help end the pain that Baxter has been perpetuating for years. To stop the exploitation of her tribe for his pleasure."

"What do you mean, 'someone like you'?"

"Someone born with supernatural gifts. Turns out, that Keyaha was also a student of the tribe's shaman. She was learning the mystical ways of her people. A secret she kept to herself."

"So, what did you do to me?" I ask, rubbing the miraculously healed wound on my previously perforated neck.

"Not a thing. That was all Keyaha." She places a hand on my shoulder and squeezes gently. "She brought you back. Healed your wounds before you left us for good." Her gaze shifts back to the road. "She healed us both."

Stating that this is a lot to absorb would be the understatement of the year. We should be dead—twice over. But it seems Keyaha's ultimate mission was to end Baxter's tyranny, to give her tribe peace, and to reunite with Nannokto in the next life.

Granting Kylie and I a third chance to live was her parting gift.

"What about Nannokto?" I ask. "He awoke inside of me. I mean, I relived both Keyaha's death and his own. Where did he go? Why didn't she bring him back into me permanently?"

"Because the Kenneh'wah were revived out of hatred, not love. Something neither Nannokto nor Keyaha believed in. Not to mention, it was the enemy—a chek-tah—that summoned them."

"Baxter."

"Yes, as well as the spirit of the Spaniard who shared space within Baxter's mind and body."

I shoot her a look.

Her gaze meets mine briefly as she says, "Just as Nannokto awoke inside you, the Spanish soldier who lead the assault on the Kenneh'wah awoke inside Baxter."

"So the fact that we were all inhabited by these spirits . . . does that mean we were all—" I make quotes with my fingers "—human radios?"

Kylie shakes her head. "Using the necklace as the power source, Baxter forced the shaman to turn the Kenneh'wah grounds into a spiritual doorway of sorts. Recycling the fallen warriors with new victims, who, upon death, would physically and mentally transform over time into more Kenneh'wah hunters. An endless supply of bloodshed to satisfy Baxter's palette for the death of innocents." She chuckles and says, "However, the shaman threw a monkey-wrench into Baxter's game."

"He did?"

"Yep." Kylie points at herself with her thumb. "Me."

"But how?" I ask as the pounding headache in my brain makes itself very known.

"When the shaman picked up on my intent to kill myself, he inadvertently found himself a fellow shaman, sha-woman, whatever you want to call me. With me in the game, via my death, I revived Keyaha who was able to put an end to this nightmare." She glances at me briefly once more with those beautiful eyes of hers and says, "She did so by granting her people sleep and much deserved eternal peace . . . and by taking their rage and giving it to Baxter."

"That's why your hands were glowing?" I ask. "Why the warriors fell as you touched them?"

"As she and I touched them, yeah."

"Right."

"I know it's a lot, Rodney. And trust me when I say, I get it. I'm still trying to digest this myself," she says as she shakes her head in disbelief. "But through Keyaha, I felt every ounce of pain, every ounce of loss for those who were slaughtered that fateful day—from her father to her lover."

I stare at her in quiet awe, as a tear forms at the corner of her eye and slips down her cheek. I reach over and wipe it away. She turns to face me, eyes sparkling with more tears. I'm taken aback at how a woman with such a tough exterior has let down a little bit of that wall. Just enough to show her true emotion.

"I realize how precious life is," Kylie continues. "And how selfish I was to even consider taking my own."

I nod, feeling the exact same way. By the generosity of a forlorn spirit, I've been given a second chance at life.

Technically a third.

That goes for both of us.

I reach over and take her hand, squeezing it, grateful that it is not covered in blood or gore and is very much alive. "I agree."

Up ahead is the on-ramp for I-95. Kylie throws on the blinker and merges onto the highway, entering in a river of speeding cars, trucks, and semis. A road sign tells us that Miami is roughly an hour away.

I've never been so happy to see traffic.

To see life once more.

And Miami is the opposite of where we just were.

Speaking of which, I ask, "So, being that we were in the middle of nowhere, how do you know how to get to Miami?"

Kylie gestures toward the backseat.

"What?" I ask.

"Take a look."

I turn in my seat to find two garbage bags.

"The one on the right," she tells me.

I open it up to find a bunch of wallets and purses. ID cards, driver's licenses, and cell phones. The former belongings of the victims who were reluctantly sucked into Baxter's game.

When I turn back to look at her, she's holding up a cell phone. "God bless iPhones," she says, jiggling the phone in the air. "Got about 12 percent battery left. Just enough to pull up the map app and lead us out of the Everglades."

The Everglades.

Son of a bitch.

That makes sense. Talk about remote. With an area roughly half the

217

size of Rhode Island and a population of around five hundred people, remote is the perfect word for it.

"While I left you to recover in the truck, I ransacked Baxter's trailer," she says. "In one of the bedrooms, I was horrified at what I found."

"What?"

"Over a half-dozen boxes of what's in the bag." She glances at me for a moment. "Rodney, some of those cardboard boxes were old. Stuffed with victims' belongings from decades ago."

The thought of hundreds of people, being plucked from their lives or misdirected here makes me feel sick.

"Can you imagine how long this has been going on?" Kylie asks. "Baxter using a tour bus to trick people into his game."

I am imagining this.

But then I'm struck with another thought. Who's to say that using a fake tour bus company was the only way Baxter lured people into his game? Maybe it started with kidnapping? Or any other means by which to prey on individuals who were at the end of their wits.

"Imagine," I say, "people go missing every day."

"Not today," Kylie says as she lays a hand over mine—the hand that's holding the bag. "When we get to Miami, I'm taking these to the cops. We're going to give a lot of families some closure."

I nod in agreement. It's a somber, heavy duty but it must be done for the sake of the families and in honor of the deceased.

"And using the map app, I dropped a pin on the exact location of Baxter's camp so we can let the authorities know," she says as she squeezes my hand. "Hopefully between the police and local Native American tribes, they'll be able to recover some of the remains of Baxter's victims and formally identify the Kenneh'wah's burial site. Or at least recognize where their village once stood."

I glance back at the other bag. "And what's in there? More of the same."

She shoots me a look, then adjusts herself in her seat. "See for yourself."

I set down the one bag and grab the second. It's heavy as a sack of books. When I open it, my jaw drops. "Jesus." I shoot her a look of shock. "How much is in here?"

"I don't know," she says with a smirk. "But it's a lot. And that's not all of it."

"There was more?"

"Damn right, there was." Kylie shakes her head. "Baxter had a big safe. Full of money he either stole from his victims or got from pawning off any jewelry or valuables they had. I took one stack of bills for everyone who died on our bus."

"What are you planning on doing with this? I mean, you're not going to keep it all, are you?"

She makes a face in disgust. "Oh God no."

"So what's your plan, then?"

"I snapped photos of everyone's IDs from the garbage bag. Again, it was the folks who were all riding with us, save for Mr. Grimm and dear Damien." Traffic continues to build, congesting the highway. "Let's just say that their families will be receiving anonymous cashier's checks in the mail at some point, courtesy of Baxter." Kylie's eyes meet mine. There's a flash of anger deep within them as she says, "It's the least that asshole can do after what he did to them and their loved ones." She shifts her gaze back to the road. "I left the rest of the money there. For the authorities to sort through. Like I said, it was a big safe."

"On that note, I think we should make sure that Bear's family is the first on that list to receive payment," I say. "Along with a note telling them how much he loved them."

There's a pause, then Kylie nods. "Agreed."

As the sun sinks below the western horizon, I'm grateful knowing that doesn't mean the hunters will be chasing us down. It just means the inevitable end of this day and the beginning of a new one.

"Anything else is on the agenda?" I ask.

She fishes out the gem'kah necklace from her pocket. Dangles it from her finger. "We're going to drop this off at a friend's house—actually the same place I'll most likely crash, too."

"Why not just keep it?"

"Two reasons," Kylie says. "First, the longer it is in my possession, the more it will begin to consume me. That old anger will reawaken, and the fallen Kenneh'wah will resurface, ready to fight."

"That doesn't sound like a bad deal. Not if you can control them. You've got a bit of Keyaha in you, right?"

"It's not something I want to risk finding out." Kylie sighs. "Let's just say, there would need to be an end-of-the-world reason for me to awaken them again."

"OK. So what's the second reason for getting rid of the necklace?"

"We don't need another Baxter getting ahold of it. Or a Damien."

"You mean Rupert," I say with a scoff.

"Either."

"So, who is this friend of yours that you're going to give the necklace to?" I ask.

"Her name's Amanda. We've been buddies since kindergarten. I trust her with my life and know that she'll dispose of the necklace properly."

"Uhh . . . what is she? Some kind of museum curator?"

Kylie smiles and shakes her head. "Not exactly. Let's just say she works for a secret organization whose specialty is collecting rare religious and spiritual artifacts and protecting them from society as a whole." She takes her eyes off the road as she says, "And we both know what society has the potential to do when given power undeserving to them." She gives me a little nudge. "Maybe I'll take you along with me to meet her."

"I'd like that."

"OK, but don't mention anything about the whole secret organization thing," she says. "It's not exactly common knowledge."

"It's not like anyone would believe me anyway." I laugh. "I mean I'm still not sure how the cops are going to find the story about reincarnated tribal warriors hunting people as live entertainment for a sadistic voyeur."

"Well, maybe we don't have to tell them all of that. There were several men on Baxter's team, including Baxter himself who carried out the deeds." Kylie shrugs. "Besides, it's not like we have to prove our case. We're the victims here."

"What about the money you took?" I ask. "You know there are cameras everywhere. The cops could replay the footage of you emptying out part of the safe. By the way, how exactly did you open the safe?"

Kylie grins from ear to ear. Drums her fingers on the steering wheel. "I didn't." Shoots a thumb over her shoulder. "Baxter did. Keyaha and I made him into our little puppet. Got him to help us load the bag with money, then erase the last few hours of footage. It's all on him. His little world finally collapsing on him."

"And then what happened to Baxter?"

"So, you mentioned mojitos before." She glances in my direction, one eyebrow raised as she asks, "You like mojitos?"

"Um . . . sure."

"OK, how about I tell you the rest over drinks?"

"Are you asking me out on a date?" I ask, suddenly feeling euphoric.

"I'm not asking you out. I just want a drink. Bad."

Can't say I disagree. Though the thought of exploring something more with Kylie would be amazing. I wonder if she feels the same? Guess time will tell. At least we're both very much alive to find out. I still can't believe that we survived that ordeal.

But we did.

And here we are, cruising down I-95 in a dead man's pimped-out truck. Both of us reeking of sweat and dirt. Neither one of us caring because it feels good to be alive. Whether it's a second chance at our first life or our second.

Or technically our third.

"OK," I say. "Mojitos it is."

"Good. And by the way . . ." Kylie glances in my direction. "Thanks for never giving up and fighting for me until the end. No one has ever done that for me."

I chuckle as I say, "Honestly, who saved who? As bizarre as this all is, I wouldn't be here if not for you."

"Or Keyaha and Nannokto."

Guess she's right about that.

I take a moment and close my eyes. An overwhelming sense of peace fills me. I feel reborn again. The desire to snuff out my life over trivial crap has . . . evaporated.

When I reopen my eyes, I catch sight of the moon, outlined in a soft, white halo. No eerie red glow to be found anywhere. In the distance, the Miami skyline shimmers as if it were made of crystal.

Miami.

My new home.

I look at Kylie. Her face beaming. She catches me out of the corner of her eye and winks at me once more. If Baxter inadvertently did one thing positive in his life, it's bringing Kylie and me together.

For now, I'm just grateful to be in her company, no longer under supernatural or man-made duress, and headed, hopefully, to a fresh start. We both smell like a locker room and look like ass, but right now I couldn't care less. If I could, I'd squeeze her hand, bring it up to my lips, and kiss her dirty, blood-stained knuckles.

But not wanting Kylie to clock me for an unwanted gesture, I restrain myself. Instead, I ask her, "So what happened to Baxter?"

"I really wanted to tell you over drinks because I am a big fan of toasting." Kylie laughs to herself. "But then again, after what we've been through, I doubt a drink will do much."

"A big fan of toasting, huh? OK," I say as I twist in my seat to face her. My curiosity is piqued. "Let's pretend we're already parked at a bar, mojitos in hand, Michael Bublé is playing in the background. What would you want to toast to?"

"How did you know I like Michael Bublé?"

"Um, Keyaha told me."

"Cute," she says with a smirk.

"It was a lucky guess, all right?" I feign that I'm holding a drink my hand. "So . . . what would you toast to?"

Traffic slows to a grinding halt on I-95. Kylie glances in my direction. The red haze of a hundred taillights outlining the soft features of her face.

Kylie raises an imaginary glass. "A toast." She bumps her hand against mine. "To karma."

A chuckle escapes me as I answer, "And here's to never riding a bus again."

Acknowledgements

Had it not been for my team of beta readers, The Death Wish Game would've been an entirely different book. I owe a debt of gratitude to my good friends Grant Johnson, Christopher Dotson, Ryan Sargent, and Serena Fisher. I was content with the first few drafts, but I felt that it could have been better, though I couldn't figure out what exactly was needed to take it to the next level. Thankfully with their feedback, the professional editorial eyes of Joanne Gledhill and Jim Spivey, and a lot of coffee, I transformed The Death Wish Game from something I was content with into something I am proud of.

The Death Wish Game was supposed to be the fourth tale in my short story collection, Nightmares in Analog. I wanted to take a break and do something different after spending two years on Faith Against the Wolves. I felt a short story as a bookend to Nightmares would have been just the thing.

Sixty thousand words later, and my next novel, The Death Wish Game, came to be.

This story just refused to be confined, and as I wrote it, it just kept going and going with no immediate end in sight. Sometimes you just have to let the story tell itself, and in this case, it did just that. I began writing it August 2015. I had always wanted to do a story about a group of passengers unknowingly destined for a bus ride to Hell—I just didn't know what that Hell was. Once I got knee-deep into the story, I found out. The story unraveled itself as I wrote it and I honestly felt like one of the passengers witnessing the horror unfold all around them.

Like every story I have written, the urge to give up is always there.

Self-doubt and self-judgment seem to be on par with writing, but once I have completed something and see that it has impacted others in a positive way – whether by the sheer enjoyment of reading or the opportunity to be a part of my journey as an author – I am grateful that I never gave up.

Thank you for being a part of that journey, and I sincerely hope you enjoyed The Death Wish Game. Now . . . onto the next book!

Jonathan Chateau
July 11, 2017

A Note on Suicide

While The Death Wish Game is entirely fictional, suicide is not. We all go through dark times and rough patches, but suicide should never be an option. If you or someone you love are exhibiting the warning signs or having thoughts of suicide, then it's time to do something about it. While none of us can control our circumstances, we are responsible for how we react to them.

I am no expert on this topic, but having experienced the assistance of my local crisis center, I was able to help save someone close to me. They are there to listen. They are there to help.

Please don't wait.

To find your local crisis center, click on the link below or contact the National Suicide Prevention Center directly.

National Suicide Prevention Lifeline: 1-800-273-8255

Crisis Center Locations:
https://suicidepreventionlifeline.org/our-network/#section-1

Suicide Warning Signs:
https://suicidepreventionlifeline.org/how-we-can-all-prevent-suicide/

About the Author

Jonathan Chateau grew up reading books by Stephen King, Dean Koontz, and Michael Crichton. However, it was *Fight Club*—both the 1996 novel by Chuck Palahniuk and the 1999 film by David Fincher—that inspired him to pursue writing.

Currently, he has completed three novels: *Faith Against the Wolves, Nightmares in Analog,* and *The Death Wish Game.*

When Jonathan's not writing, he's wandering the aisles of Home Depot, painting Warhammer & Walking Dead miniatures, jamming out to My Chemical Romance, or spending time with family and friends.

He resides in Tampa, Florida.

Find out more about him at www.JChateau.com

Made in the USA
Columbia, SC
05 November 2017